Australian Gothic

—

P.S. Clinen

Also by P.S. Clinen:

Tenebrae Manor

A Boy Named Art

The Will of the Wisp

Vignettes – An Anthology

Trick Shots – The Lyrics of Pinnacle Tricks

Patina #1

AUTHOR'S NOTE

This novel is a work of fiction. The characters and incidents portrayed herein are of the author's imagination. Any resemblance to actual persons, living or dead, is entirely coincidental. This novel deals with heavy themes that some readers may find distressing – including scenes of trauma, death and loss, mental health illnesses, suicide and self-harm, domestic abuse and violence. Great care has been taken to ensure such themes are presented in a manner that upholds the respect and tact that they deserve; however, reader discretion is advised.

For GOD and family.

ONE

Sunday, 10 August 2025

Logistically speaking, his father had died at a convenient time. A downturn in project work had seen employees who had accumulated excessive leave sent on a conscripted sojourn. This, coupled with a recently serviced car – the same second-hand Toyota Corolla he'd bought in June 2007 – meant that Locrian Smythe had acquired a new reason to get lost somewhere old. It was news of a deceased patriarch that now saw him careening down the Princes Highway, but four new tyres certainly helped the situation as well. Nobody knew that he had left Sydney. Locrian had tried to inform his manager; the phone call had been as awkward as any other tete-a-tete shared between them;

"It's who?"

"It's Locky Smythe, sir,"

"Locky. Drop the 'sir', mate, c'mon. Look, if you're calling about your last pay cheque, the girls in HR are working on it. Problem at the bank or something. I don't know; I'm just the messenger,"

"Was just saying – or wanted to say – I'll be away for a few days out of town. If that's ok."

"Right. Mate, you're on leave. I don't care what you do, bud. Where to? Should hit up somewhere warm, relax, you know?"

"Southern Highlands, actually. To Dad's place. Or his old place. He died, yeah,"

"Oh, shit mate I'm sorry. But mate, why are you telling me? You do what you need to do."

There wasn't anything he needed to do though. His sister Leah was the executor of the will, and it had only been a delay on her end that saw Locrian head to Major's Crossing in her stead. It had actually been Locrian who had suggested it, with Leah reluctantly agreeing, whilst imploring she'd only be a few days behind. Locrian hadn't asked her why she'd be held up. Leah didn't ask why Locrian had offered to help. It didn't matter.

The August sun set early, and so had begun its descent by the time Locrian turned onto the Kings Highway at Batemans and headed inland away from the sea. The Great Dividing Range cut its sawtooth peaks into the amber sunlight, and it was difficult for him to recall what day of the week it was. The lack of working routine had made it so, and yet he knew it must have been the weekend because of the footy match playing out on the radio. A cold wind met him from the south, flitting the sepia grass in a turgid swell bespeckled with a golden afternoon sun. The eucalypt shivered at the wind's caress, towering in ancient silence all about the roadside, and Locrian's maudlin trance was shifting to frustration as the radio signal shuddered in and out. Truthfully, he'd been driving too long, and would do well to stop to stretch his legs and refresh himself. Braidwood wasn't too far off now; from there it was only another hour or so drive to his father's property. It was a small town, Braidwood, a couple of thousand residents tops – at one stage Locrian might have called himself one of them, but that was far further back in time than he often cared to remember.

The Corolla ambled past a decrepit sign marking the entrance to the town. The few people who walked the streets looked in his direction with accusing eyes; or at least it seemed that way to Locrian. In reality the car passed too quickly to discern proper expression, but he was often one to assume negative intent in others. Still, there remained the feeling of heads turning; of wide, sparsely animated streets; a stray dog wandered aimlessly about; cockatoos ransacked a garbage dumpster foolishly left open by a shop owner; and curtained house windows illuminated pockets of living rooms with an indifferent glow in the increasing dusk.

As he pulled into the petrol station, Locrian turned the headlights of the car on, before realising he'd need to turn them off again immediately anyway. The ignition cut, and the silence that struck was palpable; the radio may have dropped out miles earlier, but Locrian had left the console on, and only now in the shivering quiet did he realise he'd been hearing that buzz of static for a solid hour. His cheeks tingled; he felt the blood in his veins pulse menacingly in his temples.

The attendant was an older looking man, so slouched in his chair behind the counter that he seemed melded to it, as if he had come with the place when they bought it. Sightlessly he worked the eftpos machine with his eyes fixed on a television screen in the corner playing the same football match Locrian had attempted to listen to in the car.

"Pump two, on card,"

"Sixty-seven today, mate,"

"Port up?"

"Nah, Freo by a kick,"

"Bastards."

"Still time."

It didn't matter. Sport was like life – getting so invested in these small pockets of time, only to forget them almost immediately. In the heat of the game, winning or losing was the only relevant focus, but there'd be nobody who'd still remember some random match between Port Adelaide and Fremantle in the years to come. Small pockets of time – wasn't all of life like that?

Awash with a swathe of embered orange and bruised lilac, the sky began its nightly exchange of lanterns as the western sky grew dimmer, the sun passing the torch, as it were, to the silver moon coin emerging in the east. Grief was easier to find at the day's end; Locrian fought back the welling heat of tears as he continued on his way with the morbid realisation that nobody awaited his arrival at the property. He decided that the distraction of a short detour around town might settle his nerves. Braidwood was different, yet entirely the same in the way that childhood haunts are upon revisiting; it startled him to see how small everything looked. The old Catholic church that had once towered over him in awe as a child now seemed ruinous; a park that had once seemed an untouched frontier now little more than a hectare of grass where an old statue of a miner stood vigil beneath a line of poorly manicured oak trees.

An acrid odour of petrol had spilt onto Locrian's hands, intruding on his thoughts despite his best attempts to ignore it. He pulled up out the front of a small grocery store and searched in vain for a spigot or fountain – *anything* – where he might wash his hands. No matter; he'd buy some hand soap, and maybe something to eat while he was at it. He recognised Gymnopedie No.1 playing softly in the store, and thought it to be such a strange place to hear a piece like that. The simple melody helped though; words were too much to bear at the present moment. The harmony waltzed slowly from D major to minor as he perused the aisles, his focus dropping in and out much like the radio signal from earlier; the light battens casting their fluorescent beams on the colourful and reflective plastic of various wares.

Food, right.

Concentration was difficult, and he was in no mood to make any sort of decision. Grabbing the basics of a small grocery shop, he hesitated for a brief moment before a packet of peanut butter pretzels. Normally he'd do his best to avoid eating anything he would deem unhealthy, especially after he had taken to long-distance running in his early thirties, but tonight could be different. There would be no parent to tell him to eat his vegetables first, and that sad thought made him vehemently stuff the packet into the basket and proceed to the counter. A weary clerk added up his wares while her daughter sat behind her running a pencil over the staff lines of some sheet music – *Gymnopedies by Erik Satie.*

So that's why that piece was playing – this girl must be studying it.

"Practice well," Locrian smiled.

Both mother and daughter curled a corner of their mouths in a sort of half smile; between the two they'd have a whole.

"I do my best to teach her," the clerk replied.

"It's important," said Locrian, not entirely sure what he meant by that. He was the only one who considered it though; the clerk had finished the transaction and returned to helping her daughter whilst he slipped out of the store.

The clock beamed twenty-five minutes to seven in orange and black as the Corolla curled back onto the road, out the southern side of Braidwood. With any luck he'd pull up at his father's property at half past seven. There had been no change to the chill wind, but now in the darkness of the evening the temperature had plummeted considerably. It was a cheap heating system in Locrian's car, groaning in protest as he aimed the vents towards the steering wheel where his hands clung tightly. The warmth was worth the lingering smell of fuel blowing into his face, as he turned off the main road onto the dirt trail that wound through the bushland forests of Major's Crossing.

There was no township here, just a smattering of dwellings across plains of farmland, interspersed with forest of both Australian natives that grew bedraggled, and the conifers that grew erect and sentinel for a nearby logging company that used the colder climate to grow such pines. In fact, nothing of note (with exception to a small hamlet by the name of Captain's Flat) could be seen anywhere between here and Canberra. Locrian already knew that the isolation had suited his dad – just enough interaction with the outside world to raise two *reasonably* functional children was all he had required, and once Leah and Locky had grown up and out, well, he had been free to vanish within himself ever further.

The road dipped and turned, tossing him this way and that as the car struggled over the uneven terrain – it wasn't a car built for any sort of off-road venturing; he felt his chest tighten at this mild annoyance, for this part of the drive required a focus that he was unwilling to conjure; he desired a return to the flat highway where his mind could drift. Instead, he decided to take in the surroundings as best he could (although the darkness now made it almost impossible to see), as it had been years now since he'd last made the trip down to his childhood home, and much the same as Braidwood, the surroundings felt paradoxically familiar yet alien. He crossed the weir which in times past had flooded under heavy rain and prevented him and his sister from attending school; it had obviously been a dry few months of late, since the creek was little more than a sluggish trickle over weed-strewn rocks. A barbed-wire fence would then hug the trail, stopping livestock straying away from their properties where they might be at the mercy of reckless drivers that often passed by much too quickly.

Presently he found himself on a straight stretch of road that tumbled downhill, and Locrian spotted a dark shape on the road ahead of him;

A rock?

Perhaps it had tumbled down the slope and onto the road. But no, this was different, and as he drew closer, he realised it had to be some sort of creature – a wombat – that blocked the way forward. Locrian pulled the handbrake on with a crunch and stepped out of the car, the headlights illuminating the furry beast that lay dead on the dirt road. He nudged the thing with his foot, despite already knowing it no longer lived; it yielded somewhat to the touch of his boot before gravity rocked it softly back into its slumped position.

Poor thing, some bastard's hit you, haven't they?

It was hardly an unusual occurrence, yet Locrian still found himself pitying the creature as though he'd known it personally.

"Too much death," he sighed to no-one.

He nudged it again with his foot, applying more pressure this time to see if he could shift the body off the road. It would need to be moved before he could proceed – wombats were heavy creatures, and this one was a monster of a thing; no matter how hard he tried, he couldn't move it with his feet; he'd have to try something else. Locrian looked around for a thick branch he might use to use to lever under the wombat, but the night had descended and he could see no further than the headlights of the car.

"Fuck," he hissed through his teeth.

The trunk of the car was popped open and he began to rummage about for a solution. The wheel jack might have worked had it have been longer, and the only other objects in the car besides his duffel bag were a bunch of old towels covered in engine oil. He would have to use his hands and shove the beast off the road himself. Residing to the fact that his hands were already soiled by traces of petrol, he placed a begrimed towel across the wombat's broad back and pushed. The beast was heavy – much heavier than Locrian had anticipated, and only after several minutes of exertion was he able to roll the corpse onto the dried grass by the roadside. It rolled onto its back as Locrian stumbled forward, almost crashing on top of the thing. When he had gathered himself, he caught sight of the joey that lay still in the pouch of the wombat.

So, it had been a mother.

Locrian felt his heart flash with grief as he staggered backwards and choked back a sob. He observed the smaller creature in vain, but knew it to be dead – there was no denying it. Around him the night was silent; the nightjars had ceased their song; the engine hummed as it idled in the darkness, and the doomed creature at his feet would never move again.

How long had he stood there? It can't have been longer than a few minutes; the cold discreetly seized Locrian's arms in a frigid embrace, and his breath hung in the air in staccato puffs. Above him, a cauldron of bats flew northward, screeching off into the distant sky and shaking him from his trance; he could no longer look at the mother and child. He walked to the other side of the road and plucked a handful of twigs from a shrub, laying two of them in a cross-shape on the wombat pair; someone would be around to spray-paint the same shape on the corpse eventually – it was done to confirm passers-by that no joey had been left alive near the dead parent. Then, feeling a little silly for doing so, Locrian lay two more sticks in the shape of a crucifix next to them, before deciding against it and kicking the sticks away.

"Stupid," he muttered; head down and sniffing, he steadily recomposed himself.

He threw the towel back into the boot of the car, knowing he'd probably end up throwing it away now anyway, before sitting back behind the driving wheel and resuming the final leg of his journey. It was perhaps less than ten minutes later that he rounded a steep corner where, hidden amongst the trees, he spied the familiar metal gate and mailbox that marked the entrance to his father's property.

TWO

During the night, he dreamed. He dreamed that he feared death. Now a man may consider a fear of death to be a natural reaction without truly considering the indifferent finality of the scythe, and the guttural terror it represents. Locrian could see a hospital ceiling in his mind's eye; the checkerboard beige of tiles dotted with light battens, and the back-and-forth of nurses bustling. They didn't care for his plight; to them he was a commodity, an object of another day at work – little more than a task. He imagined that he was surrounded by loved ones – the children he never had, the parents who had already shuffled off the mortal coil, the lover who had taken her own life – and none of them could do anything to prevent the fate that would soon reveal itself in its own time; they could simply watch as though behind glass. Locrian was to undergo heart surgery – or maybe brain – something serious and intricate, and he was overwhelmed with fear of the anaesthesia. Would he awaken in recovery as though no time had passed at all? Or would he close his eyes for the final time oblivious to the notion he'd never wake again? That instinctual call to survive, so primal in its impact, drove his heart into a frenzy; he felt himself little more than a rat consumed by amygdalic darkness, a mote of carbon dust in the cosmic void.

The sound of wind chimes echoed a sonorous bell-call, crying out from just behind the veil, a veil that reveal itself to be the curtains of his father's living room. Locrian lay upon the sofa lounge, looking down at the valleys and peaks of the blanket contorting to his body; at the full-length windows that lined the northern face of the old home; *at the shadow of the figure that glided formless outside.* The wind threw itself up the valley towards the house on the hill, carrying with it an impossible cold – the cold of death that hung in swathes about her form, and Locrian, paralysed in a half-sleeping stupor, saw his desire reborn as a terrible spectre that patiently tried each window for ingress.

Her.

The word caught in his chest in a stuttered exhale, a sickly little thing held against him like a wounded creature. Her white hand presented a limply pointed finger that dragged along the panes, the languid scrape of her nail on the glass like a branch swaying in a storm. The night bleached black as her fingers traced in wonder, beckoning him to approach.

Come, she said.

Her name bulged in his throat; mechanically he rose and approached the window, where he felt himself locked in her tiger gaze. The frost crept about the window until those eyes were all he could see, and he found himself outside his father's property, standing where she had just been. The wind had dropped to hint at a distant storm silently flashing its lightning in an intermittent pulse. There was no sound; there was no colour, and the cold tightened its grip on him. Frost skulked into the soles of his feet that crunched through the grasses encircling the house. He wandered in a trance, a somnambulant night walker intruding on the still scene. In the witching hour darkness, he might have been the only human being of heat for miles. His icy hallucination appeared before him whenever he looked, although for whatever reason he could have navigated the hillside blind at that point. When he stepped over hillock and burrow, he'd look up and see her further on up the incline, closer still to the rear of the property, where the tallest eucalypt trees reached blasphemously for the heavens.

Impatiently he scrambled further up the hill, replacing one breath with another, one heartbeat for the next; over and again he stumbled on tree roots and lichen-bitten boulders. There was a worn path that ran between the trees at the top of the hill, winding towards a barbed-wire fence where Locrian could see the Mercury eyes of the spectre staring back at him; feel the Jupiter lies of her deception —

how could he know what was real anymore? She guarded something there, something stationed at the fence at the rear of the property. The approaching thunder finally bellowed in the distance.

THREE

October 2021

Hers was an icy love that purged, sharp as mint, the years of hostility that had built a tall pyre in his heart. A love comforting and alien – the nights of Neptune, the heart on Pluto – who could know it? He hated to drink; hated the burn in his chest (and coffee was better, anyway), but in her he could release himself to the intoxication of her moon-scented beauty. She first appeared to him in an Annandale pub; October 2021, the furthest he'd travelled since the pandemic-enforced lockdowns were lifted, after some four months of isolation. It was strange to see so many people gathered in mirth; stranger still that this dusky jewel would put aside the time to speak with him of all people.

"Your parents called you 'Locrian?'"

"They must have had a *hippy* phase, I guess,"

"Why not 'Dorian?' It's right there as a legitimate boy's name and still musical,"

"That's what I've always said. But hey, 'Locky' is pretty normal,"

"But who'd want to be normal, right?"

"I think an ordinary name can lead people to have ordinary expectations of themselves,"

"Ooh, deep. But not yours," she teased, "that's from a movie,"

He stuttered.

"That stop-motion movie! God what was it called? I know, I'll call you 'Mr. Flat-Five',"

That most dissonant of musical modes – *Locrian* – the tritone against the tonic; this girl must know her stuff.

"You play?"

"Not so much anymore," she said, "I burnt my hands a while back and can't fret the strings too well,"

"Guitar? I only know a few chords. I was always more piano. And hey why 'flat-five?' I think I'd prefer 'sharp-four',"

"Nope," she smiled, "that would be me. I'm Lydia,"

He rolled his eyes, "Lydian mode; you're joking right? Far prettier than my namesake,"

"Naturally, but still nice and unstable,"

"Let me get you a drink," he laughed.

"You wouldn't know what to order,"

"I prefer my coffee; but I'll get you whatever you want,"

"Then I'll join you. Something with milk though, please."

It wasn't a traditionally Australian custom to have coffee in the evening, really more of a European thing, and some more rowdy locals might have sniggered behind their beers at the fancy fella over there with his coffee. Locrian couldn't care less though, he was used to being a bit of an outcast, and happy enough to be amongst the commotion of the busy pub after so long indoors alone. The band had started their set, belting out some Powderfinger songs, and now moved on to an old Nick Cave tune. Those who preferred sport glued their eyes to the television screens showing a rugby league match, where the Kangaroos were smashing some team Locky didn't recognise. He'd come alone, and wasn't sure why. Surely after such a long time spent social-distancing he'd have craved the company of his few mates; but no, he couldn't do that yet. Better to ease himself back into the whole 'friends' thing – he'd always struggled to make and keep them.

"Ok," the bartender swung by, "Two coffees. For you, sir,"

"Thanks,"

"And one for your imaginary friend,"

"Steady on!"

The bartender had left before Locrian could properly register the insult; he looked over to Lydia and tried to laugh it off.

"Is it that unbelievable that a woman like you would sit with me?"

"What kind of woman would that be?"

Locrian blushed, "Oh come on," he stammered.

"Relax, Mr. Flat-Five,"

"Still not sure about that nickname,"

"No more confusing that spelling 'Smythe' with a 'y'"

"I didn't tell you my last name,"

"Lucky guess, ordinary name,"

"We're talking an awful lot about me," said Locrian, "what about you? Are you here with friends? A partner?"

"Nope. Just wanted to get out of the house. The most exciting thing that's happened to me in the last four months was Aunty Gladys dropping by on the daily,"

Locky laughed, "Yep! That's a sad routine that I think we all did; watching the premier announcing how many new sick people we had in the state. My friends would message the group chat – how many cases today? Or more importantly – what colour coat would she wear today?"

"Blue coat meant good news,"

"Of course, she was lib. Can't be seen wearing that nasty Labor red,"

Lydia laughed in turn, "You're a funny one, Mr. Flat-Five. But what's your wife going to think when she hears you've been flirting with girls at the pub?"

"No wife," said Locrian, "and is this flirting? You approached me,"

"You invited me to sit down,"

He took a sip of his espresso, "Nope, thirty-three and no wife as of yet. Thirty-three and a half if you want to get into semantics. Jesus was dying for our sins at this age; what am I doing?"

"You're sitting here talking to me,"

"Then I guess miracles do happen… Shit, that was truly awful,"

"It was," she smiled, "if that's your best, definitely better to say you aren't flirting,"

His heart was racing; what was it his father said about something being too good to be true? He tossed back the last of his coffee but realised that wouldn't quell his rapid heartbeat.

"Are you going to drink your coffee?" he asked.

"After you, dear," she said, "milk coffee is always better taken after the shot,"

"Right,"

"So, I found you here alone too. What about your family? Friends? City's back open,"

"Dad's down south," he said, "my sis is in Adelaide; haven't seen her for a few years now. And doesn't look likely soon either with the borders closed,"

"It's stupid, right? We're a giant island, why close off parts of it?"

"Yep,"

"Well, borders won't stay closed forever," she had finished her coffee and now stood up, "how about I be your stand-in friend until then?"

She was leaving; he had to do something before she slipped from his grasp forever.

"Okay, h-how will I find you?"

"On the socials, Mr. Flat-Five – look me up. I'll be around town as well, you'll see me."

Locrian watched her leave, sauntering unhurried between the pub patrons who paid her no mind; for the first time since he couldn't remember when, he felt an immediate pull to another human being. He had to see her again, even if it forsook every other relationship he'd ever had.

FOUR

December 1993

"He starts school next month,"

"The young man; that's a big milestone. What are your thoughts on that?"

"Excited. Worried," he paused, "He's ready – my son. I think another year at his grandmother's might not be stimulating enough,"

"Your mother still watches them?"

"She's amazing; probably deserves to enjoy her retirement but she's back watching my two on weekdays. I always try to get them as early as I can, but you know – work,"

"A difficult balance,"

"Yeah; and I mean sometimes she'll come to us. That way the kids are in their own home, and if I work late,"

"And Leah?"

"Loves her big brother. She'll miss him being there during the day,"

Charlot Smith sat back in his chair, allowing the familiar teal-coloured walls of the office to wash over him and calm his breathing. Dr. Antony appeared disinterested, although Charlot knew that to be untrue; the doctor had a knack for holding space, allowing the silence to expend itself until words were necessary. In the corner, a small dog sneezed before sighing itself back to sleep – Mitzi – Charlot had never once petted her. He could appreciate dogs from a distance, but wasn't fond on patting them; some deep-seeded paranoia about unclean hands couldn't be shaken from his mind. He pondered the true value of support animals for a moment, before deciding that it wasn't his place to denounce the concept as frivolous.

"You just," he continued, "like, should they be apart? Should I be apart from them? You wonder how much time we should spend separate,"

Dr. Antony stopped writing for a moment and considered, "as much as they can bear, I think. You need to work to provide for their basic needs; and you can pour your efforts into their emotional needs at any moment you can,"

"I do think about that; like how they'd be sick of me if I was a 'helicopter' parent. I see them every morning when they wake up, and I tuck them into bed every night,"

"Exactly; and they'd know to expect that from you, Charles. Kids are resilient, they draw confidence from you every time you turn up for them. No matter how hard their day could be, you can be the consistency they need,"

"Stuff like hardship, like how metal gets stronger when tempered, put under stress; I get it. But how much suffering should they have to endure? What kind of father am I to have let them seen so much, this young?"

"Put it another way – how much of their suffering is under your control? To suffer is to be human, this is an unfortunate reality we face. As parents we can only shield them so much, and sometimes it isn't about preventing bad things from happening, but standing behind our children so that when they look for help during life's hardships, well, 'there's Dad. Dad's got my back.' It bears mention that they might not even remember anything happening now when they're older; they're still very young."

Charles could feel the tears behind his eyes press forward; he scratched at the bridge of his nose and blinked heavily. He realised how cold his hands felt; hear the unseasonably cold wind blowing in the morning sun outside the window; feel how utterly exhausted he was, and would love nothing more than to curl back into bed and sleep forever. Dr. Antony didn't break the silence – he never did.

"I suppose," Charles said, "I'm just worried now with school, about my boy, how he'll be different. The other kids will be like 'where's your mum?' How is he supposed to handle that?"

"You're no longer seeing that new woman, right? I think you told me that a few sessions ago,"

"Oh, no, not anymore. Saw her for about six or seven months say; but it didn't work out. I don't think I was ready; she understood. It was pretty mutual,"

"Not a bad result then, I'd say,"

"No, not at all. I think the kids might miss her? But they haven't mentioned her at all to be fair,"

"Well, back to our original thought here – there are a lot of reasons why a person might not have both parents in their life; divorce, death, adoption. None of these things are that uncommon; I'm sure your son won't be alone."

Outside, a wind gust battered the signage with a dull thud. The green leaves of the trees held tenaciously to their branches and Charles could have sworn he could hear wind chimes somewhere.

FIVE

Monday, 11 August 2025

Awakening was never easy. No matter the hours that had passed, be they of any quality or quantity, a groggy miasma of sluggish inertia clung to Locrian like so many cobwebs. He was aware of the cold, aware that it had troubled him for the entire night, and despite there being simple solutions to his malady, he lay languid in the bone-cold dawn, listening to the wind chimes that had plagued his dreams. A window had been left open, and he was unsure if it had been he who had done this, or if he had neglected to notice it upon his late arrival the previous evening.

Dad, close the window.

But no-one would respond; he was alone, and any voices that weren't his own were nothing but chemical impulses triggering memories in his brain.

Close that door, Leah. Do we live in a tent?

The door slammed.

Without the attitude, please.

Locky left it open.

And I'm asking you to close it, thank you.

The curtains fluttered restlessly until he clasped the window shut, and they returned to their inert vigil, the call of the wind chimes becoming muffled. There was a claw-like tear in the flyscreen (his father hadn't ever replaced them), and through this sinister incision Locrian observed the crisp morning, the frost-cloaked grass glistening in the dawn, the magpies warbling glissando, and the vast valley that stretched out from his father's old house on the hill.

"I thank God for another day,"

He muttered his mantra every morning he could remember, though some days it was more difficult than others. Today he was undecided; the tragedy of his father's passing had lent him a cloak of understandable melancholy, yet for a moment amongst the icy glass of morning, after the wind-tossed nightmares of the evening past, Locrian allowed this moment's respite to shiver down his spine and raise his shoulders somewhat.

The house was a ramshackle edifice; rustic and roughshod in its construction, pertaining somewhat to the artisanal style of homes found in the bushlands of Australia. Timber and rust abound, it propped itself up on old bones of ironbark, surveying the hillside from a perch halfway up the slope. Here its wooden façade and corrugated tin roof had weathered the gusts of the highland winters and the scorching horror of its summer sun alike. Although it stood two storeys tall, it was not a large residence, and most of the ground floor was occupied by a combined kitchen and living room, where every other room seemed like an afterthought tacked onto the façade – a mudroom along the southern side; a study to the west; and on the eastern side, next to the kitchen no less, was a bathroom. The location of the water tanks was the most likely reasoning behind this bizarre set-up, and Locrian recalled the awkward feeling of showering while his father or sister were cooking food on the other side of the wall.

Although he had returned to his childhood home many times in the past, he was always struck by how much larger he felt; he had experienced a similar feeling in Braidwood the day before, a giant stamping around a toy-block scene. He wondered what Leah would think of it, what memories she'd stoke when she arrived, for she had moved to Adelaide upon the threshold of adulthood; as for Locrian, it had been some five years gone since he'd last made the trip down from Sydney. Locky shuffled to the kitchen with the moribund reflections of his past glinting dimly in the recesses of his mind. He was thankful to see the refrigerator had been emptied of perishables – either a neighbour must have done it or perhaps his father had anticipated his own demise. Yet his dad hadn't been so old – sixty-seven to be said – and he had always been a man of sturdy health, although perhaps his stoicism had hidden a submerged torment of body.

It fascinated Locky to observe the pastoral picture of his father's kitchen and ponder; ponder the final movements of the old man; the lid of the coffee jar screwed on for the last time; the plates stacked neatly on their rack, never to be used again. With a magician's precision he thoughtfully slid a few coffee cups about in the side cupboard, though it really didn't matter which one he took for himself. For a moment his gaze fell on an ugly mug, misshapen and deformed, and recognised it as the Father's Day gift he'd made in the second grade. He felt his grief emerge once more as he clutched the sad little thing; the stains ringing the bottom of it belied the amount of use his father had gotten from it – Locrian could not believe he'd kept it for so long. He put the cup back; he couldn't look at it again.

The crunch of the coffee beans skittered into the grinder, and the rising aroma was reward in itself. Hand over lever, white knuckles curled – those modern automatic grinders could never compete, good coffee was always worth working for. Counter-clockwise he turned it, filling the drawer with caffeinated stardust. Locrian thought of 'clockwise', and how the 'right' way to turn seemed at odds with the very cosmos itself – for man knew that the Earth spun in the opposite direction, and the planets too – *gauche*. If that wasn't the perfect allegory of humanity's defiance against God, he didn't know what was.

He was not expected in Goulburn until mid-morning, and the drive would take him about an hour. Locky was almost grateful for the troubled night's sleep, as his early rising would allow him to take his time. The cold morning air sank its fangs into him as he slipped the glass doors of the living room open and stepped out onto the patio, his breath intwined with the rising steam of his coffee. It was a stunning scene - blissfully quiet, only the birds and the wind intruded upon the silence. The valley had not yet shed the blue residue of the dawning and would not take on its greens and browns until the sun climbed a little higher. Locrian's feet felt frozen, yet he found the sensation to be rather exhilarating; when struck by the cold, he was reminded of his position as a creature of blood – *alive*.

How could it be that such a paradisial scene foreshadowed the tasks that lay before him? The immediate arrangement of his father's affairs; and beyond, an uncertain future where the man who'd acted anchor for Locky would no longer be there. When he considered this, the pleasant house on the hill took on a sinister air, the dawn hues of blue and violet concealing pernicious intent. This was little more than a Potemkin village – a charlatan ready to unravel at the first pluck of loose thread. He turned his head to the sound of an owl, who'd clearly stayed up later than its brethren, and gazed up the slope to the trees that towered at the summit. Recalling his dream, Locky furrowed his brow to observe the divots interspersing the grass in a clumsy line following the incline – footprints – the trail dotted back to the house to where they terminated at his own muddy boots, inside beside the sofa bed. Had he gone wandering in his sleep? Surely not; he'd never been somnambulant before, at least not to his knowledge, yet the vivid recollection of the spectre he'd seen and the undeniable trail he'd left of his own volition left no doubt. Yet he'd vehemently deny anything of the supernatural. He could certainly attribute a bout of somnambulance to the heavy nature of the situation; and the apparition? – a mere hallucination; his anima haunting his dreams.

Still though, he thought he might explore the top of the hill later that afternoon.

The coffee had gone cold, yet he drank it anyway, clinging to its promise of vivacity like it were a life raft. Turning himself inside he stood in silence for a moment and breathed deeply of the creaking timber of his old home, the familiar smell, the aura of its void; it was a house that had swallowed many secrets, and taunted of buried joy and horror alike. It was distinctly uncomfortable to be in a place from his past, as though he were intruding on old grounds where he no longer belonged,

We know Locky the child, this is his place — who are you?

The stairwell to the second floor wound itself up from the living room into a sort of loft where three bedrooms lay. The twisted steps creaked beneath his feet as he ascended this trunk to canopy. There was an anteroom at the summit of the steps, where the ceiling sloped and a large skylight threw sunbeams across the dust motes that floated ad infinitum. His father had set up his telescope there, alongside a rather decrepit chair that looked almost comical next to the opulent brass of the device. Locrian had always disliked the position of his bedroom lining up directly across from the stairs, as he'd lay in bed with a direct view of the unknown that might lurk just a few steps below. To him, either there was something there, or nothing at all, and both ideas terrified him as a boy.

These days there was nothing orderly about the bedroom – his father had used his children's vacated bedrooms as little more than storage spaces. In fact, the entirety of the second floor gave off the impression that it had not been in use in many years, perhaps his father had migrated to the more accessible parts of the house in his advancing age. Locky's bedroom was the worst offender, having gained walls within walls as furniture and boxes were stacked haphazardly; he could liken its traversal to the Minotaur's labyrinth. Remaining though was a ruinous piano, the same one that Locky had spent hours playing in his childhood, too big to move with him when he'd rented his first flat in Sydney after his eighteenth birthday. A paisley-patterned rug had done little to prevent the dust mounted on the instrument, which groaned as he lifted the lid to reveal the yellowed ivory keys beneath. A rush of nostalgia flew over him; no doubt he'd be woefully out of practice, having switched from playing music in recent years to merely writing it.

It had stimulated different parts of his brain to learn his theory, and aside from the occasional strum on his old acoustic guitar, Locky hadn't played anything musically for what felt like an eternity. He let his fingers glide lightly across the keys before depressing one of them – a B note – and he knew already that the piano was horribly out of tune. Pressing each second key in a line he sounded out a D, F and A, forming a dissonant half-diminished chord made all the more jarring by the tuning of the instrument. The sound was monstrous after the years of reticence, and he didn't care enough to give the chord a resolution – any other tonality would have done the trick – the tonic chord of his namesake was left to hang in the room where dust and decay had taken root. He would play no more, needed no reassurance of his ability or knowledge; he'd long since given up the need to impress or prove to anybody, including himself. Maybe now that he'd soon be disposing of his father's possessions, he could finally move the piano to his flat and start playing consistently again. Or maybe he'd just let it go along with the rest of the junk. Locrian couldn't ever decide what was worth keeping and what should be forgotten.

There was no reason for him to venture into his sister's old room, for it was of similar ilk – lined from floor to ceiling with boxes. The anteroom at the top of the stairs held the only area of seemingly lived-in space – a few square metres where his father had set up the telescope. The warmth that radiated from this sunny corner almost had Locky smiling; a star chart and notepad crowded a small coffee table where an unwashed coffee cup sat – his father must have sat there very recently. The chair strategically aligned with the flue that rose from the fireplace downstairs; the heat radiating off the steel chimney would have been pleasant to the old man on winter evenings. For Locrian, he'd held an aversion to the chimney, having once burned his hand on its surface as a child.

The star maps made no sense to him; the cosmos had always fascinated him, although he'd never had the patience to learn the nuances the way his dad had. It was a fiddly, intricate hobby; one that suited his dad perfectly; but for Locky, spending painstaking minutes lining up the telescope on a dot of light millions of miles away simply didn't hold as much thrill.

You can't even see the rings properly.

Sure you can. You can see them right there, look.

Clearer pictures in books though.

Pfft, you kids. No appreciation. That there is a planet ten times the diameter of Earth, you're looking at it!

Weird how it's so small to us.

That's because it's so far away. Consider that distance. It's awe-inspiring. And to think the next planet in line after that is twice as far away; can't even be seen without a telescope. It lay in darkness until we first saw it recently — 1700's, son.

Why do you like this stuff so much?

His dad paused and thought, Because it grounds me, mate. There's a duplicity to it that I can't get my head around. That we're so small, yet so special. So insignificant, so miraculous. An insignificant miracle, there's no other way to put it.

Profound.

You're sarcastic now, Lock. You're young. But it's true. And some people lean more into insignificance; some choose to read more into the miraculous. One way is definitely easier than the other.

SIX

December 2021

"When's your birthday?"

"June 7th,"

"Gemini! I knew it,"

"You don't actually believe in that shit, do you?"

"Well, if you want to believe in me, you've got to get into it a bit," she laughed, "You've got to love me for all my pissy little quirks,"

"I suppose I'm not one to dictate on reality,"

"If I can blame the more unsavoury traits of my personality on the way the stars were when I was born, I'll do it,"

"Fine, I'll bite. What are you?"

"Libra," she said proudly, "Balanced. Just. An even pairing,"

"And nothing unsavoury, right?"

In those first few months together, Lydia would visit him in his Erskineville flat, above the coffee house that became a makeshift jazz bar in the evenings. Locrian could not help but feel a little embarrassed by the cheap paint of his rented walls, the propensity to rising damp and the uncouth street noises of the weekend's drunkards. But Lydia preferred the solitude it provided them, and despite desiring to break free of his home after the pandemic lockdowns, Locrian felt in no position to resist any request from the icy love, the dusky angel that had entered his life. He feared that she might disappear at any moment, such was her flighty charisma; that she might discover just how boring he was, and he was willing to overlook any and every imperfection she might harbour in her sylvan heart. They had enough in common to bond fast, and their disagreements made for great discussion. Both were adamant that Pink Floyd were a better group when Syd Barrett was there, and even though their most prolific work was released after the talismanic front man had left, it was either inspired by or directed about him. Lydia didn't believe that Robert Smith would ever get around to releasing another album, to which Locrian rebutted,

"He has said it exists! Has a title and everything,"

"*Songs of a Lost World?* Lost album more like. Just because someone says something is real, doesn't mean it is. He does this all the time – every album from The Cure is that last one, then it releases and 'next one will be out in six or seven months'; it's a total cock-tease,"

Their latest love had been St. Vincent, whose chameleon collage of music had them drawing comparisons to the late, great David Bowie.

"I'd say you even look like Annie Clark," he'd said.

"If you say so," Lydia shrugged.

It was usually the same band in the café most Saturday nights, and boy and girl would leave the windows open to the dying year's breeze as serviceable renditions of old jazz standards rose to meet them – Miles Davis; Herbie Hancock; Wayne Shorter; and Lydia's favourite – John Coltrane's *A Love Supreme*. Locrian wistfully closed his eyes and listened as Lydia eyed him with a smile.

"I owe much of the music in my life to my dad," he had said, "he's got like a million records,"

"I'll be sure to thank him,"

"He'd love this flat for that reason; dingy though it might be,"

"He's never visited?"

"I suppose not. Are you close to your family?"

"They're around," she said, "I should definitely make more effort."

When he looked at her, he saw a full moon when he was ebb; she the wax to his wane. He would throw everything to her if he could; worship her, but he knew he shouldn't come on too strong. In so many ways, he wanted to propound her as family. He could and would give her all that he had, but that wouldn't be what she'd want. Her Lydian harmony, his Locrian dissonance; he walked the high wires, yearning to drink of all she was but afraid to know her better and shatter the illusion. For that first stage, anything was plausible. She could be perfect, Venus – and why not? – they put their best selves at the centre stage of their courtship; where he performed his pathetic bower bird waltz and presented desperate trinkets of affection while she watched with a magpie fascination.

What was your childhood like?

What did you want to be when you grew up?

None of that mattered to them; just she, Lydia, as she had always been, even before Locky had known her; and he with all his insecurity and anxiety, perfectly acceptable by the grace of her curiosity.

Sharing the same work hours meant they'd meet together in the evenings and on weekends, but occasionally they'd take their lunch breaks at the same time and rendezvous in Hyde Park where, under the spires of St. Mary's cathedral, they would converse amongst the filtered shadows of weeping fig. Most of the time the benches would be found occupied, and other office workers sprawled on the lawns, so the two of them would instead saunter in no particular direction, past gatherings of ibis (Lydia called them 'bin chickens') and street fundraisers (Locky called them 'charity muggers') – both could prove as irritating as the other. But they had each other; she with her knack for scaring away the chuggers with wry remarks while he would chase the birds until they flew, much to Lydia's chagrin of laughter mixed with cringing. Locrian wasn't afraid to unveil the mirthful side of his personality when in the company of a woman who gave him the time of day, and sure, bystanders might have stared, but the thrill of her smile was worth any blushes.

"Is this how you usually impress the opposite sex?" she asked.

"Just the ones who would listen," he quipped.

"I could have had lunch with friends; but here I am watching a man-child chase birds,"

His heart leapt; he had meant to be humorous, but fretted now that he may have destroyed any shred of respect she might have developed for him. She held him in a state of despair that felt eternal, before finally softening,

"Relax, Flat-Five; I'm joking,"

Emboldened by the reprieve, he said, "You can call me by my name, you know,"

How could he be his authentic self and not risk deterring her? He could have just walked into the sea or have the ground swallow him up. And yet, to offer up an ideal forgery of appeal instead? No – that would be worse; he'd always been told that truth trumped any lie, and that any deception a man might present was found out in time. And how could he feel the love of another if he played a charlatan hiding his true self? He would have to continue the tightrope walk.

It was Lydia's turn to lighten the mood, "Well, you told me your name is Locrian. I'll bet not many call you Flat-Five,"

"Most people wouldn't understand the connection,"

"Fine," she smiled, "Locky."

They had reached Archibald Fountain, and sat upon its edge; children ran about in the sunshine, trying to land themselves in the path of the fountain spray that blew with the light summer breeze. A busker played his guitar in the shade, pleading for coin with an impressive rendition of a Nick Drake song.

"He can play," said Lydia.

"These kids can too," replied Locky, "do you ever think other people just have more fun that you?"

She pulled a strand of hair from her face, "Yeah. I think. When the sun is this bright, and end of the year is here. I think about whether I'm missing something; like how others seem to make friends easier than me. Or that they might actually enjoy being with their families at Christmas, that the whole thing isn't a complete emotional drag,"

The cathedral bells ran out the quarter hour and sent the ibis and a few seagulls into flight.

"I've been trying to be more open to new people," said Locrian, "you know, since the lockdowns ended. It was a long time to be alone. I worry that I won't keep up any sort of momentum, that you'll just see me sink into my usual boring self and won't want anything to do with me,"

Lydia put her hand on his knee, "you're clearly an emotional person, Locky. I look at you and I don't see anything fake. I see someone who does in fact want to be seen, even though you're pretty reserved,"

Locky felt maudlin on a sudden, "I should just get a grip. You're so amazing, I just want to be good enough; I've never had a woman give me this sort of attention, actually approach me. I'm not used to it, I guess. In my head I suppose I've been with a lot of women; I tend to fall in love with any girl who even looks at me. But this is different, and I'm trying hard to not hide away in my shell,"

"But you're worried I'm not going to like you? That's silly; I already said I could have had lunch with friends instead. I choose to come here because I like being around you. I get what you mean though, I think I probably mould myself to whatever suitable personality might suit a guy I'm with; when I'm myself, they say I'm just pretentious,"

"Well, I hope your true self is the kind of person who'd wilfully be around a guy like me,"

She laughed, "What have they called me? 'Manic pixie', 'dream girl' – shit like that. I was manic long before those terms even existed!"

"Now *that's* pretentious," laughed Locky.

Lydia leaned over and kissed his cheek, "That's me. And you shouldn't be so hard on yourself,"

"I'll keep being me if you keep being you,"

"Deal, Flat-Five – Locky, I mean."

SEVEN

May 1998

Even by the time she'd turned seven, she already possessed a Sisyphean pneuma of the world-weary; a carrying of a burden well beyond her lot. At such a young age she did not have the words or even the meaning of what formed in her developing mind. That which may have been simply kismet was to her still a map to be deciphered; a path to be chosen and trodden. And yet part of her knew she'd have to make the pilgrimage alone as the 'girl' who would like to one day become 'woman'. It was easier for her brother – he still had Dad, a celestial anchor of sorts for navigating the waters of boyhood. Leah would have to chart the course without a solid visage in the mind, rather an El Dorado that could have looked like anything for all she knew.

There was Nan, of course, whom she loved dearly; however, the generational gulf between them was one that the two of them struggled to bridge at times. There was something decidedly masculine about Leah's grandmother; she smoked feverishly, for one; a trait that often triggered quite a turn of mood for her brother Locky, and Leah definitely hated the smell too. Aside that one vice, her Nan loved a beer on a Saturday afternoon, tuning the radio to whatever sporting event was taking place –

it didn't matter what. It was the plight of the Goulburn girl, perhaps, that a peculiar ruggedness cloaked the hardy residents of that hinterland town, and while Leah had the tight bond typically shared by grandparent and grandchild, her Nanna wasn't someone she aspired to emulate. To gather her wisdom, the morals to her fables – these things were fine, it was just that Leah could never see herself getting so cranky simply because the Canberra Raiders had won a game that she'd placed a bet on.

The road between Goulburn and Braidwood changed names, depending upon which way one travelled, and it was every second Friday that Ruth would make the hour's drive to pick up her grandkids from school and whisk them back to her house on Kinghorne Street. For Leah and Locky, it was their second home, and most of the time they wouldn't have it any other way. Nan was looser with the rules than Dad, and Goulburn offered a *mildly* livelier scene than their quiet home in Major's Crossing. Other times though, when the exhaustion of the school week overcame them, they'd complain of homesickness, that Dad was just at home 'doing nothin''. It wasn't until the pair were much older that they realised these weekends were the only chance Charles got to upkeep the many other facets of his life to provide for his two young children, or that grandmothers were a treasure only for childhood that would be lost sooner than one could ever want. It was true that it took a village to raise a child, and Ruth delivered a city for her son.

The flurried silhouette of her brother was quickly distancing itself from her, so Leah swung the plastic grocery bag over her shoulder and jolted off the footpath into the laneway. If she was going to beat Locky home, she'd have to try a shortcut. The asphalt was dotted with puddles from the day's earlier drizzle, but now the sun had returned for a twilight encore, illuminating the cold afternoon with brilliant shades of orange and pink. Winter foretold of its arrival with its chilled tendrils in the early sundown − for it was barely five o'clock in the afternoon, and the night would soon be undeniable. Leah panted as her feet pounded the ground, and wooden fences flowed past her as she ran. A flock of cockatoos screeched overhead and the cold pricked her skin as it mingled with the heat of her core that lay trapped in a thermal jacket. She made it to the backyard of Nan's house and flew down the side, almost tripping on the garden hose in the process. But there he was, her brother, arms akimbo, standing triumphant on the front porch,

"Beat you,"

"Don't care," she snipped, dropping the grocery bag.

"I even had two bags to carry,"

"I said I don't care!"

It was difficult for her to win any sort of verbal scuffle with her brother; he was almost three years older than her, nearly double digits; she just wasn't smart enough. Leah hated being the younger sibling – always chasing, always trailing. She bent to readjust the carton of milk and the packet of biscuits, before standing upright with a grin and pointing at him,

"First the worst!"

"Nope. Zero the hero,"

Nanna finally caught up, rummaging through a set of house keys with a bag on each arm,

"You kids are too quick; leaving your grandmother in the dust,"

"Nan, Locky teased me,"

"Leah can you please fix that bag, the chips are getting crushed,"

"I said Locky teased me,"

"Nobody tease anybody," said Ruth, "Locky be kind to your sister, she's still little."

They bustled inside and set about warming the place for the evening ahead; on went the electric blankets; the radiator that sat in the old unused fireplace; and into the beanbag chairs went brother and sister with the ABC cartoons blaring from the television set. It was all baby shows until six (so said Locky; Leah agreed with him to save face, but secretly loved them – *still little, indeed!*), then it was The Simpsons and Neighbours (grown-up shows); Sale of the Century came on at seven and that meant they'd begin winding down for bed. The two shared a room when they stayed at Nan's, and Ruth had long grown to accept that the kids would fall asleep later than usual on these nights – the temptation to chatter was too much, and besides – there was no school in the morning.

Leah nuzzled into her beanbag and inhaled the smells of garlic and onions as her grandmother began cooking dinner. It was these moments, wrapped in the warmth of a familiar place, while the night was kept safely outside, that she would ache longingly for in her adulthood. How could she have understood the importance of this mundane Friday night until hindsight had a chance to make entrance?

"Who's playing tonight, Nan?" asked Locky.

"Newcastle and Norths, mate," she called from the kitchen.

"Boo Knights! When are the Sharks?"

"Tomorrow. Broncos,"

"We'll get 'em. Get 'em back for the grand final,"

"Let's hope so, Lock; they've won their last three, so we can be confident,"

"Gosh Nan, I know,"

None of it made sense to Leah, she just listened with her thumb in her mouth. Everyone told her to stop – *you're too old to do that now;* although many gave her lenience given the unusual set-up of their family life.

"Can we stay up and watch Sharks?" she asked.

"No Leah, they're tomorrow," said Locky.

"We'll see, love. Might be a bit late for you," Ruth understood what she had meant.

Leah didn't care about the game, just the chance to stay up a bit later. She heard the tap of the wooden spoon on the edge of the pan and Nan's hands clap together,

"Well, there's some washing out on the line, guys. I'll be outside for a moment if you need me."

Leah wasn't really watching the television but staring vacantly through it; it had been a long week at school and she was tired. She listened to her brother noisily chewing away at a bowl of chips; the sizzling of the meat that slowly cooked on the stove; the faint ticking of the clock on the wall. The screen door presently opened again and a rush of cold shocked her back from reverie.

"Would you kids like to see something?" called Nan from the back door.

Leah leapt up immediately, "Let's go Locky,"

"No thank you."

She thought nothing of his response and went out into the backyard, aware of the cold concrete steps under her bare feet. Nan was standing next to the clothesline with her eyes to the sky, which had turned to a deep indigo washed with the barest strip of amber on the western horizon.

"Locky didn't want to,"

"That's ok, love. Take a look there; what can you see?"

She gazed past Nan's pointed finger to a bright star that watched silently from its astral perch. There wasn't much to be said of it; it was a star alright, the only one she could see at this time, but it was still early.

"That," said Nan, "is the evening star,"

Leah was puzzled, "Aren't they all evening stars?"

Nan laughed, "You're gorgeous, girl; I suppose you're right. It's what we call a wandering star,"

"But it's not moving,"

"It is, just very slowly. It's a planet; that's Venus,"

"So small,"

"That's just because it's very far away; but it's always the first star you'll see at night,"

Leah stood and looked, her grandmother's hand resting on her shoulder.

"When you see Venus," her Nan said, "you might like to think it's Mum looking down on you,"

"Is that because Mum's far away now?"

"Yes, love. It's just a nice thing you can think about when you see the night sky. She loved you endlessly."

Leah felt strange; she'd never known her mother. She was aware that mum had been around when she was a baby, but that was far too early in her life for her to remember anything about her. To her, it had always been her father and brother, and Nanna lived in a different house. It was peculiar to hear that someone she couldn't remember had loved her so much. *Venus, Mum watching out for us* – she'd remember to tell her brother later.

EIGHT

Monday, 11 August 2025

The road had changed its name as he entered Goulburn. The house had new owners in the years since his grandmother had died. Parked across the road from the old home on Kinghorne Street, Locrian sat behind the wheel lost in reverie. It was true that new owners lived here, but the house itself stood unchanged. Still the dark brick of the walls; the pillars that held the front porch; the mailbox on a post knocked to a slight angle. That wasn't his Nanna's car in the driveway of course, and like a stranger spotted reading your favourite book on the train – this felt like a backhanded insult, an invasion of privacy. Why couldn't he call this his home anymore; why did another have any right to lay claim of what he'd had first? Notwithstanding others who would have owned the house before his grandmother did; this was an interrogation of the psyche; he could see it no other way. As long as it meant something to him, it would exist as his own; as long as he clung to the love he had for his Nan, she would endure in memory. How horrifying to realise a day would come when everyone who had ever known him would be gone. The house might still stand, the plot of land that bound it remain with the turning of the Earth, but he reduced to a name in a book nobody would read; a grave nobody would visit; joined to his ancestry in the silence of death, blind to one another's presence in an eternal nothingness. The call of the void was spoken in whispers barely heard, and promised nothing that faith hoped for. He wondered where his memories went when he'd forgotten them.

Locrian considered the frightening idea that he was now the oldest living member of his family – not that many remained – he and his sister and her daughter. Would he cease to exist if nobody remembered him? He missed Leah on a sudden, as though she were a capstone to his very existence, and despite her imminent arrival he needed a touchstone of reality to ground him from his turbulent nihilism.

The house is exactly the same.

The phone made a soft zooming tone as the message was sent – a quick photo taken too. He had no desire to draw attention from passers-by by suspiciously snapping pictures of a stranger's home; the key turned and the tyres crunched on the gravel.

Lock.

Yeah Dad.

It's about Nan.

I know.

She's gone, mate.

I know.

It was peaceful.

Are you ok? (What a stupid thing to have asked).

Fine. I'm fine; sad (his speech quickened); Leah's fine, but sad. And I love you. And I'll talk to you soon, my little son (his voice broke).

Locky could not recall the rest of the conversation. He remembered being struck by the moniker of 'little son', and could relive the numbness he had felt upon receiving that call. Dad certainly had spoken to him again, innumerable times in the thirteen years between his and Nan's passing, but now he would never again.

The logistics of a man's death could not have been more foreign to him. Though he was a mawkish man who considered mortality somewhat regularly, Locrian realised that he had not the faintest clue as to what happens when a person dies. A question many ask and none can answer is where does the soul go when we exit this plane – few stop to consider more prosaic questions of what to do with the body, now useless; the possessions, now homeless; the house, now shell. Assiduity would not make way for grief, dashing that snowdrift aside and pushing onwards.

An old steam locomotive trundled along the line that skirted the east edge of town where the funeral home stood, itself a vestige of colonial Australia. It was modest in its opulence; a sandstone building adorned with timber veneer shutters and a corrugated iron awning. With few cars on the streets that Monday; the haunted bellow of the train; the smoke from its chimney, Locrian thought he might have stepped back in time. Wrestling with thoughts of an era lived and gone, he felt a tearful nostalgia for a life he never actually lived himself.

The fitout of the building was modern and stark; walls were painted a dizzying white, synthetic plants either side of the reception desk like a veritable funeral altar – the only thing missing was the coffin. He could have chuckled wryly at the sight of the dust that had collected on the stitched leaves of potted palms – *death dressed up as life* – how ironic it all seemed. Locrian caught himself before descending into a vindictive sarcasm; more likely he was just trying to protect himself from pangs of his broken heart.

"Good morning," came the voice of the receptionist, who sat small behind a curved computer monitor.

"Hello," his voice stumbled; he realised he hadn't spoken to another person since the day before, "my dad is here, I think; his body I mean,"

The woman smiled patiently, "Of course, let me get someone along to assist you, Mr –?"

"Smythe, with a 'y'."

She left him alone in the room as he stared at the patch of sunlight on floor, the only thing in the room that was brighter than the walls. He became aware of jazz music playing softly from speakers in the ceiling corners and resolutely shook his head to ward off any intrusive thoughts. For a moment he thought he saw the visage of a woman staring at him through the window but realised that couldn't be the case – the patch of sunlight was perfectly shaped to the window's dimension and the sun's pitch.

Locky's loco – stop thinking about trains.

His mind was everywhere and nowhere at once.

"Lachlan Smith?"

He turned to face an older woman in a suit, hair pulled tightly in a bun.

"Locky is fine," he corrected.

"Right this way," she smiled.

She led him down a hallway that wouldn't have looked out of place in a family home; the building must have been converted from a residence to a business. Floorboards creaked beneath their steps as they entered a room not dissimilar to the front reception, where the undertaker had set up a rather pleasant workspace.

Dealing with death all day long, probably best to make it as comfortable as possible. Or is this to make me more comfortable? Death dressed up as life.

She tapped away at her computer for a moment before turning to him with the same sugary smile plastered on the receptionist.

"Right then Mr. Smith; I'm Esther, I'm a funeral director here. How are you feeling today?"

Pleasantries, understandable.

"I'm ok, about as ok as I can be, I suppose,"

"Of course. Now I always like to open by saying we're here for you in this difficult time and deeply sorry for your loss,"

"Thanks."

Thanks?!

"And if there is anything specific you need along the way, please do let us know,"

"I'll probably have plenty of questions; I don't really know what to do,"

"No troubles at all, Mr. Smith. Well, we believe we have your father here with us; now I understand this can be a challenge, but we're just going to need a confirmation of identity before we can issue the death certificate,"

"Wow, you get a certificate? That's kind of funny,"

"Yes, perhaps not the type of certificate you might get at school, but yes,"

"So, will this be like the movies? You take me to some cold refrigerator room and pull on the right drawer?"

He hated himself for defending with humour, but could think of nothing else to say – *how much small talk was acceptable at a time like this?*

Esther laughed, "No, not like the movies at all. We don't even need to leave this room; we like to make this as gentle as possible,"

She procured a cardboard folder from the filing cabinet and begun leafing through it,

"It was a neighbour I believe who contacted us; your father lived alone?"

"Yes, I can imagine so, I'm from Sydney so didn't exactly see Dad every day,"

"Of course, I understand," she sat back down, "now I have some photographs here; our morticians take great pride in making the deceased look as natural as you might remember them, but this of course can be traumatic for some,"

"That's ok. Must be done."

Esther slid a photograph face down on the desk towards him, and he gazed emptily at it for a moment. He already knew his father was dead, his house empty, his voice silenced; but to see him now, this would confirm it beyond a doubt; he hesitated.

"Take your time," said Esther.

He rubbed his hands up and down his thighs and breathed heavily. Was this the sort of thing where it was best to rip the band-aid off, so to speak? Just look at it and be done with it? He flipped the photo over and stared for a moment at the ceiling before looking back down. Whether it be a fatigue in his body that faltered his concentration, or an overload of emotion and function, he was unable to discern exactly what he was seeing for several seconds. It was a pallid face, the sallow cheeks and closed eyes that were somewhat sunken made Locrian feel he was looking at a cheap imitation of his father; a poorly made mannequin that only slightly bared any resemblance to the strong man he'd looked up to. He slid the photo away from himself and gazed at the floor, hand on cheek. Esther patiently placed the photo back into the file and waited, holding the space while Locky composed himself.

"Is that your father, Charlot Smith?"

Locrian nodded, "Yes it's him,"

"Ok then," Esther spoke softly.

He felt he might have short-circuited; that his body would never move again, or would never want to move again; he just stared at the floor, his sight glazed over and out of focus. To do anything now just seemed pointless.

"Mr. Smith, do you need a moment?"

He cleared his throat, "No, no, all good. What happens now?"

"We will hold your father here while you and your family begin funeral preparations. Are you the executor of your father's will? Or do you know who is?"

"No, my sister actually. She was always more organised than me," he tried to laugh.

"Very well, and is she local?"

"No, South Australia. She'll be here in a day or so,"

"Ok, she will need to consult your father's will – you two might do that together,"

"Yeah, I need to get a look at it. We thought it might be at the house somewhere, but she'll know for certain,"

"Either there, or you can visit a public trust office; there is one in town you might go to, not far from here,"

"Thanks, I think there's a guy in Queanbeyan? Some solicitor guy I need to see; I might wait until my sister arrives,"

"It will be important to learn whether your father had any specific requests; as you might already know, some people choose to be buried, some cremated,"

Locrian winced on a sudden and cleared his throat again. His breathing became raspy and his eyes stung with tears. A tension crept up the back of his neck and he felt as though his heart was being squeezed by an unseen fist.

"Take your time, Mr. Smith,"

"Sorry. Just – sorry, no cremation, no,"

"My apologies; try not to fret, we're here to help you every step of the way,"

He nodded.

"We will make sure we honour your father's wishes,"

He nodded.

"And that your family is assisted to the best of our ability,"

He nodded. He nodded. He began to disassociate with the room; the white walls, the fake plants. If he just kept nodding and agreeing, this would be over soon.

NINE

April 1994

"I lost my temper with him the other day,"

"Tell me about that,"

"It was stupid; I over-reacted. I caught him playing with the cigarette lighter,"

The doctor considered, "Well, it makes sense that you'd need to chastise him about safety,"

"Stupid, really," Charles continued, "I should have put it away where he couldn't reach it. I'm supposed to protect him. I'm all he's got. Then I go and scream at him like that,"

"Every parent makes mistakes at times; hoping they're not big ones. Did he hurt himself?"

"God, no big mistakes this time,"

"Did he hurt himself?"

"Huh? No, he didn't, thankfully. Just – his face, the look – I scared him,"

"What happened after that? Did you speak to him? Explain why you reacted as such?"

"He hid in his room. I sat down with him and told him the lighter wasn't a toy, how it's dangerous and all that. He's already terrified of fire; I feel I've gone and made it worse,"

"Seeing your loved one play with fire, with something dangerous – it makes complete sense that you would react to protect him. If you're unhappy with your reaction and fear that you've hurt him, you can explain yourself when everyone has calmed down; apologise if you feel it necessary."

A short silence pervaded between them. The dog Mitzi noisily lapped at her water bowl before pensively staring at the window. Charles realised he was nodding incessantly – a broken metronome. He agreed with most things Dr. Antony parsed – he had to; how could he not? Oftentimes he felt guilty of approaching the doctor with appeals to a higher ordeal or authority, like one might approach a church altar with head bowed; in him he hoped to discover reason, that he might unveil the meaning behind his senseless suffering, because God knew he couldn't find his own path through. There were times when he assumed that the cards dealt to him were actively rigged against him – there was bad luck, but then there was Charlot Smith. Someone had to run last, no doubt, but did it always have to be him? Some cosmic prankster had tied itself to him, seen him born beneath a bad star and befallen to burdens so great. It angered him that he couldn't find the answers himself, that he had to rely on other men with university degrees to guide him.

"I never get this shit right; I just lurch from one disaster to the next. I can't change it,"

"You can influence things to a certain point –"

"I swear I'll never have a funeral. I won't put the kids through it,"

"You might change your mind about that one day,"

Charles hissed through his teeth, "God, I love Mum but why'd she go and leave her bloody lighter on the bench like that? Of course one of the kids would grab it,"

"I'm sure she wouldn't have purposefully done it; it seems an honest mistake,"

"How can you be so calm about this?"

"I can hear that you're angry; remember I am here to help you,"

"I just wish I didn't need so much help. If life would just be a little easier – just for once! I could manage alone," he said, "If I was left alone."

TEN

Monday, 11 August 2025

A triad of kangaroos grazing the bedraggled lawn scattered to the crunch of the Corolla's handbrake. Thighs aching for the hours spent driving, mouth dry from the third coffee of the day, Locrian stepped out and delighted of the fresher air; for whatever reason he'd kept the car windows closed during the drive. The jill bounded clumsily into the shrub with joey in tow, while the dominant boomer stood tall against the intruder before thinking better of it, following its syntonic spouse and minor third. Alone again under the stale mid-afternoon sun, Locky shivered to behold at the dark house, draped in the shadows of eucalypt, where it cared not for any who might have looked, its windows opaque with a blackness that told of nothing. For truly there was nothing; not the laughter of brother and sister, or the steel-string jangle of the father's guitar; just the lonely gasp of wind that past between pillars, gone before anyone could know it.

Pretend that they're married.

Pretend this is the kid.

Pretend the baby runs away (laughter).

No, no Leah; pretend that — stop laughing!

You're laughing!

Stop that baby!

Come back, baby!

There was a ragged path rolling down away from the house, away from the gravel driveway, that shifted tufts of guarded grass enroute to a small dam at the bottom of the hill; the road could be seen from here, but cars very rarely passed. The waters – disturbed only upon the surface by fingers of wind that weaved gilded sunlight into the ripples – would teem with yabbies in times past, but today would yield no catch. The entire expanse looked stagnant; his father had obviously not tended to the irrigation channels in his final days. Still though, in the creamy afternoon light it presented a scene of tranquillity that would have drifted away unseen had Locky not been there to observe it.

Myriad wildlife used the dam as a watering hole; Locrian picked his way between animal tracks to where an old crab trap lay half-submerged in the mud.

Is it a snake?

Hang on, mate; don't touch,

Don't get bitten, Daddy,

He's ok, Leah. He's an eel. Surprised he's made it all the way to our dam!

Dad gently shook the trap as the serpentine creature shifted between jolts of panic and fear-frozen stillness.

There he goes,

I don't really want to go near the water anymore.

Locrian tossed a perished tennis ball and watched it bob in the centre of the dam. Several trinkets of a past life still adorned the shore – he found an old toy boat amongst the reeds and examined it. Was this his? He couldn't remember. It seemed like something he might've played with as a child. A blue stripe was painted on its white hull, smooth under his thumbs; it stayed afloat as he set it down at the dam's edge; a relic of childhood adrift and anchorless in the wider expanse beyond the shore. Locrian turned his back to the dam and began to urinate into the nearby shrubbery. The wind carried his stream away from him (he'd made that vital analysis before relieving himself) and he washed his hands in the dam, shaking them dry in the winter air.

Never before had he experienced such mental drain. Caught in a slipstream of memory, his brain only occasionally bringing reality back to the forefront, were he able to register where he was, and why he was here. If this was true grief, then it was unlike anything he'd been led to believe; assuming that each person experienced loss differently, Locky wondered why his reaction was so hazy and muted. That horrific visage materialised in his mind's eye – his father's face – it was distressing to think that could be the final time he saw him; the next time it would likely be in a wooden pall, or maybe an urn that only hinted of its contents.

Your father is in there now.

How can that be?

Worse still was the fact that he was unable to recall exactly when he'd last seen or heard from his father. He could review his phone log, text messages; think of the time years ago when he'd last visited; but the specifics – what was the last word he'd said to him? That final turn of head as he had backed his car out of the driveway? Death stared silently and offered no answer; perhaps it was up to Locky to remember, and the fact that he didn't left him with an incorrigible regret. He sauntered uphill, following one of the creeks that flowed into the dam as the voices grew louder around him.

Is that your father?

Yes, it's him; how can that be?

A rotten log buckled beneath his tread; he reached to grab at a shoot of lantana to steady himself and let out a sharp cry as the nettles sank into his palm.

Damn fucking weeds. You don't belong.

Don't let it get you down, Flat-Five.

She'd burnt her hands in the past – that was what she'd said. Couldn't play guitar because of it. Never mind the stinging in his hand – he wasn't making music anymore.

Locky, wait.

Scrambling up a rock, he skipped over shallow pools and felt his feet press into the river sand; he could run so much faster than his sister.

Locky, I said wait!

Leah was beginning to sob with frustration; kids always did that when things weren't going their way, especially the little ones. He was almost at the top; the calls of the kookaburras growing louder,

Think it's going to rain, but it could be snow at this rate.

He wiped the blood from his hand onto his shirt, but it offered no relief from the pain.

It's a weed, mate. We have to chop it down.

But it looks nice.

Things aren't always as they seem, son.

The crest of the hill drew closer. He recognised that same alcove that had appeared in his dream; no doubt he could see it, it had always been there, he'd just remembered to give it notice. Those trees would have been planted and grown long before he was even born – why should they care if this one man paid them heed? Still the cries of his sister echoed on the wind, rustling the gum leaves, an insufferable din,

Locky, stop!

Leah, stop! That crying, I can't stand it!

You won't wait!

He was running, or at least enacting some sort of semblance of running, a sickly stagger up the hill as his mind filled the silence with a cacophony of cries,

Wait.

You won't stop me.

Wait.

Shut up!

Don't speak like that to your sister.

Wait.

A cluster of banksia trees impeded his progress, and he fought and flailed his way through the grey-green leaves while the eyes of the banksia cones stared maliciously. Bursting through into the clearing he stumbled, walking backwards, staring right back at those mad flowers; then the sound of her voice, loud, as though she were right next to him,

"Wait!"

Locrian fell to the ground with a gasp and sprawled wide-eyed on the grass. Breath came to him in short, sharp gusts; his mouth gaping for air like a caught river eel. His sister was gone, and with her too, the voices. The only sound came from the wind that swayed the wild grasses and rocked the blooms like boats on a verdant harbour. He shivered and shed hot tears from his eyes, though he was unable to say if it was grief or the inclement weather that had his eyes watering. On the other side of the incline, unseen from his father's house, the valley spread in fields of long grass pockmarked with lichen-cloaked rocks and thickets of gum trees. There was a monument there, at the crest where the hill slipped away – a headstone with the kowtowed heads of wilted blossoms at its base. Beneath a ragged veil of weeds sat an old deck chair, as though someone had sat by the grave in the past. Pulling himself to his feet – an anchor hauled from the sea, Locrian stood bewildered, trying to understand the presence of the headstone in this forgotten corner of his childhood grounds; its worn stone bore no name, or at least none that was still legible, and given its appearance of having been there for quite some time, Locky was perplexed as to who it had been erected for. He imagined his anima, the woman from his dreams, standing at the headstone; the wind carrying strands of her hair, the afternoon sun casting contrast on her profile – half lit, half shadow.

ELEVEN

Winter 2022

The weak southern hemisphere winter was rarely more than a mild annoyance; a teasing cold that couldn't even redeem itself with a decorum of snowfall; but for two introverted Sydneysiders, it was a chance to warm one another with the fanned flames of a secluded romance. Lydia moved into Locky's flat with the ease of seasoned kinship, rather than the budding and at times awkward intimacy of two who were still learning of one another. There was the tired cliché of 'feeling like one has always known', yet when it applied to them, neither Locrian or Lydia cared that they might entertain such a bored trope. For them, it was anything but; just as a weed cares not for where its seed falls, rather revelling in the delight of living at all.

She presented a complex of paradise in him; he dared to see an oasis not because Lydia was very much different to any other Australian woman in her thirties, but rather that he desired nothing more than to fill a hole in his soul, a yearning above all else to be loved without condition. Meanwhile, she saw him as a prism of light casting a spectrum of colour, where she could fill any gaps with her own primary tones. One complimented the other, and no-one would stop the ascent of two birds aloft in a double helix. Like the fog of the morning gone by midday, they moved beyond those first flirtations into an exciting new phase that shone with the promise of a warm day, where clouds that might have threatened rain were instead seen as harmonic to the pristine world they built around one another.

Above all, it was a delight to enjoy the company of another that Locrian cherished the most. In stark contrast to the previous winter, where the residents of New South Wales had been placed under lockdown due to the pandemic, he was now able to wander the streets, lungs full, upon the backdrop of his new love; even his decidedly dull office job was refreshing, and colleagues noted the change in his usually reserved demeanour. Back home, he loved to watch Lydia, fawn over the intricacies that made up her whole; the way she'd rest a pointed finger on the page of the book she read; the squint in her eyes when she brushed her teeth; the smell of her hair, or the shape of her legs when she napped on rainy afternoons. He could only pray that he offered her the same joy; yet when she opened up to him, he knew he had to be doing something right, that maybe this was a pay-off for the exhausting task of trying to be a functional human being; but no – she couldn't be a commodity, this was one of the fae who'd revealed herself to him and he had to treat it like the treasured gift it was.

"I grew up in the suburbs," she spoke softly beneath the covers, "there was this giant tree in the backyard – a camphor laurel, that had these beautiful waxy green leaves. You'd run your thumb over their surface and it was smooth as silk. And when they fell dead in the autumn, they'd turn red, then brown, then shrivel into these skitter-scatter scraps that crushed so easily in your palm. The sound they'd make when the southerly buster blew – I'd hear them outside and know I was safe because it was out there, and I was in here, in my home. It was such a shock when my dad told me it was a weed, this tree. How could something so beautiful, that meant so much to me – how could that possibly be a weed? Not a native, Dad said, and that can damage other plants trying to grow.

"Why do we say that about weeds? They thrive wherever they grow – even in cracks of concrete or the mortar of bricks. They destroy whatever pretty little flowers they can find. Isn't that just natural selection? Survival of the fittest? Anyway, I didn't care; it held me in its pull, trunk thick and roots running deep; it could've destroyed me, I wouldn't have cared. She, too big to move, held to the ground under her enormous weight; and me, this little satellite orbiting, too small to get away. That's how I saw it, anyway.

"We moved away when Mum and Dad split up, and I went to live with Dad while Mum was barely around. After that I didn't think too much of that tree. And one day we drove past my old home, and the new owners had cut it down. I can't tell you how upset I was, Lock. I cried so much in the back of the car, and Dad tried everything to comfort me; don't worry, Lydia, it's not our home anymore, not our tree, they can do what they want with their backyard. But it didn't matter, he couldn't give me what I wanted. He could speak those words, tell me it would be ok, but he could never give me my tree. Is that strange?"

Locrian just listened, watched the movement of her mouth, the tears filling her eyes, feel the heat of her breath on his face.

"Stupid, really," she said, "getting so upset over a tree,"

"No, no I understand. Please don't cry," and he held her in his arms and watched the rain glide down the windows above the bedhead.

When the weekends rolled around, they'd sleep late, rising in the mid-morning to relish the lack of plan – for neither of them liked to plot out an entire day, preferring to drift where the day took them, often wandering the streets of Newtown or Glebe until their feet ached and coffee called.

"You keep checking your phone,"

"Sorry, Lyd; it's just,"

"Your dad? Or your sister. They miss you, when are you going to see them?"

"Soon," he lied, "just finding it hard to get moving,"

Their wandering had taken them the length of Newtown, and they had circled back past a mural of the Aboriginal flag below a typographic artwork of a Martin Luther King quote.

"You should at least message them back though,"

He sighed, "Yep. Look, I know. Sometimes I just think it'd be better if I just suppressed it, even just a little. Take a step back from the past, you know?"

Lydia looked at him with concern.

"That doesn't make sense," he continued, "how do I say it – there's no point dwelling on what's already been. Better to move forward. Nostalgia is a poison,"

"But they love you, Locky – I know that much. They should still be a part of your present. You'd regret looking back one day and thinking you could have made more of an effort,"

"I guess they're just a reminder I don't care to look at. The future could be anything, all other times though – they have the potential to hurt. Nostalgia hurts – even the good memories – because they're gone; I can't hold them anymore. And the present? Well, I think we end up misinterpreting how good it actually is, and love it or hate it, this will all be nostalgia one day too,"

"That's a little depressing,"

"I don't mean it to be," he pleaded, "I guess I'm trying to say, I want to keep improving, and hanging onto the past won't do anything,"

"I think reflection is a good way to move forward," said Lydia, "but that's just my opinion,"

She was right – such realisation frustrated him. A silence fell between them for a moment; the city traffic rambled about them, and he reached for her hand.

"Look, I'll message them back. I know they worry about me; it's annoying, to be honest – like I'm some crazy bloke who needs monitoring,"

Lydia smiled, "I'd love to meet them one day; your dad, your sis,"

"I reckon you'd get along as if you'd always known one another."

They found themselves in an antique store, where vintage trinkets unfeigned and faux towered floor to ceiling, and they had to shuffle sideways at times amongst the clutter. Locky was very aware of his elbows and knees, fearing that he might bump and break some priceless artefact and incite the wrath of the proprietor, who might forbid him from leaving until the damages were paid for. Lydia, however, showed no such trepidation, seizing items in her hands like fruit in a stall, testing for ripeness with a press and poke of fingers with chipped nail polish.

"I mean, it's cute; but who buys this crap?" she whispered, holding a wooden owl figurine up for him to see, "Sixty-seven bucks!"

"Maybe don't manhandle stuff, Lyd; we can't afford to break anything,"

"But how will I know if I want to buy it?" she smirked.

He flinched as his shoulder brushed against wind chimes that hung from a coat rack, and Lydia called him over to where she was excitedly turning the lever of an old coffee grinder.

"Check this out! Old school! You will work for your coffee, Mr. Flat-Five!"

She poked him in the chest and laughed; Locrian couldn't help but smile in turn.

"Can I help you?" called the shopkeeper, who was clearly nervous about Lydia's flippant motions as well.

"Looking!" she replied, not even turning to face him.

He liked that about her – she simply didn't care what strangers thought of her; he wondered whether he could possibly master that trait himself. Wordlessly they explored, until Locrian came across an old piano that reminded him of the instrument he'd played growing up, no doubt presently gathering dust at his father's house down south. Softly pressing his right hand to the keys, he played a half-diminished chord of B, D, F, A – the dissonance of the Locrian mode that jangled in his head – why did he always gravitate to a sound so lacking in harmony? Lydia slipped in behind him and pulled him towards her, placing her left hand on the keys over F and C,

"Go again," she whispered.

Together they played their part, and a beautiful altered chord sung through the shop, her bass notes perfectly complimenting his tenor, offering a solid foundation on which to stand, and giving a complete harmony that seemed to float resolutely through the hushed atmosphere of the shop.

"Excuse me, sir," said the shopkeeper, "the sign,"

Locky looked at the laminated sheet of paper on the wall above the piano that informed prospective patrons (rather passive aggressively) to refrain from playing the piano. Lydia hid her laughter behind her hand and taunted Locky,

You got in trouble!

His face flushed with embarrassment, but he would be promptly reprieved when Lydia plonked the owl statue onto the counter before the unimpressed shopkeeper.

"I think I'll take the dumb little bird today, sir."

TWELVE

July 1994

"Charles, have you heard of the term 'radical acceptance?'"

"No,"

"I'd like to tell you a story," said Dr. Antony, "if that is ok with you,"

"Go ahead,"

"Right, now this is something told to me by another patient of mine many years ago; I retell it with his permission but of course won't mention names. And it's a story that I like to tell as an explanation of the idea of this 'radical acceptance' –

"This man was experiencing anxiety, so I had asked him to tell me of a time when he had felt himself to be truly scared, and this is what he told me; when he was a young boy, he lived on a farm with his family – nothing out of the ordinary, just a mum and dad and one brother. This farm had many irrigation channels, canals essentially, open to the air; and there were some days when this man, as a boy, liked to play with his brother in these canals. They would sit on a little raft attached to a rope, and their father would walk along the edge of the canal, pulling his boys along. Now there was a day when this was happening, that the water in the canal was more turbulent than usual – it had rained heavily the night before so the flow was quite strong. Usually the boys enjoyed this, it meant they could ride the rapids faster than normal. But anyway, the man recalled falling off the raft into the current. He was a fine swimmer, even as a child, but the water was much too strong for him to reach out and climb back onto the raft.

"Before his father was able to grab him and haul him out, he was gone, swept off down the canal towards the road, where the water travelled through a tunnel under the highway and continued out the other side. Before he knew it, he found himself holding his breath underwater inside this tunnel, still caught in the current. At this moment he tells me of a horrifying thought that came to him – at the other side of this tunnel, at the other side of the road, there was a grating across the opening, and if this were true, the boy would find himself pinned against it and unable to come out on the other side,"

"Shit," said Charles.

"Mmm, not wrong. So, his mind jumps to the conclusion *I've got to swim back out of this tunnel, or I'm going to drown against this grate;* he paddles and paddles but it's completely futile – the water pushes against him with such strength that he's unable to get himself out of this tunnel,"

"Jesus. He obviously lives if he's telling you this story? Please tell me,"

Dr. Antony stifled a chuckle, "Yes, of course, that's a necessary spoiler, I think. The boy reaches a point where he's absolutely exhausted. He's been fighting against this current but it's a battle he cannot win. His air is running out, and he just lets himself go. Stops swimming. The torrent picks him up and sends him off in the opposite direction, further into the tunnel,"

"And?"

"And the next thing he realises, two great big hands hook under his armpits and pull him out of the water. His father, on the other side of the road, waited for his son to appear, and managed to get him to shore,"

"But the grate?"

"There was no grate,"

A moment of silence hung in the air.

"The boy *thought* there was a grate blocking the way, that was how he remembered it, but he was mistaken. His father was able to rescue him only because he stopped trying to fight a battle he was never going to win. He radically accepted that he wasn't strong enough to swim against the tide and in that way, was saved,"

"What if there was a grate there?"

"Well, he probably would have drowned, wouldn't he?"

"I don't understand,"

"It is a difficult concept to wrap your head around. Radical acceptance involves realising you are fighting a battle you cannot win; that 'fate will unwind as it must'. I use this story as an example because in simple terms, it shows someone fighting against a natural order before accepting things beyond their control.

"Now he could have died in that incident, certainly. But would swimming against the rapid have done anything to change that? No. In fact, he'd have almost certainly drowned if he had kept swimming. It doesn't mean he shouldn't have tried though! Don't get me wrong there, we should always try to manage our own path, see if there is a way through, but ultimately there will be things in life that you have absolutely no power to change or control. We do well to 'radically accept' these things,"

"I think I know why you've told me this,"

"Good, that's excellent."

THIRTEEN

Tuesday, 12 August 2025

During the night, he dreamed. He dreamed of the other rooms. This was a dream he had experienced many times before, and although the semantics were always different, the theme remained the same — there were *other places* in this dream. Another room might be discovered tacked onto his home, through a door where before there was only wall; perhaps a second storey was revealed, one that nobody knew about or used; or a bedroom awaiting repair, filled with spare furniture and storage.

There was always the shock of discovering another room, the question of why he always forgot of its existence. At times it might only have a single entry point via a crawl space of sorts, where no normal human being could ever hope to squeeze through — and yet these rooms were often furnished with objects that had to have been transported in there through some impossible means.

Strangers and friends alike would mention the other rooms, sparking memories he wasn't sure were his, nostalgia for something he'd never experienced; he could see a road, a street, a path that surely led to the other rooms, and he knew that if he followed that path, he'd arrive there in time. That knowledge had revealed itself to him – because he'd been there before; he was sure of it. But there was always an urgency about getting there, for he was only there for a day, and had best make the most of the opportunity. To his chagrin, or sometimes delight, he had to travel by foot, and most of the time his dream would end before he arrived.

In an evening of mangroves, far from his home, he couldn't remember where he had parked or if he'd driven at all. It wasn't too far to walk this time, but he'd hurt his foot, or lost his keys, or maybe he'd never owned a car at all.

Entire cities might go unseen, empty of visitors, or there would be adjacent streets he could take in lieu of his usual route, just to confirm their tangibility, close the loop, complete the circuit, walk the power lines with thunderous steps. He hated himself but loved his own disparaged panache. He knew one day he'd fall with a deafening crash.

FOURTEEN

November 2001

More than one indicator told her this wasn't an ordinary weekend; by four o'clock she was certain. Sounds of bickering had rocked the house all day, her father and brother, and Leah found solace in the confines of her bedroom, emerging only for food and a subtle sneak at what was going on. She didn't know why Locky and Dad were fighting, only that it happened a lot ever since her brother had started high school. The young buck was testing the old bull – pushing for a hierarchical change of echelon that was bound to happen before long, yet perhaps Locky challenged the boundaries too early. It was easier to not get involved; her attempts to appease fell on deaf ears, and truly she was weary of the yelling.

She would lay on her bed, letting her head flop over the edge, so that everything around her was upside-down, and she could trick her brain into believing she was stuck to the ceiling. The crimson wallpaper with the little birds on it; there they were flying upside-down. The light globe bloomed from the centre of the floor, a modern miniature of a firepit, and water damage stains might be little islands on a sea of white house paint. She ran her hands through her hanging hair, fingers catching in the knots, and in the mirror against the opposite wall she envisaged herself as an electrocuted echidna. The sounds of arguments had ceased before lunchtime, presumably the father and son sulked in their respective havens; Locky drawing in his room, Dad poking about outside in his garage workshop, while Leah had just whiled the hours away reading books.

Only when hunger and boredom overtook did she gather herself up, toss her book aside and head downstairs,

"Dad, can we have dinner yet?"

But the figure sitting at the kitchen bench was not her father, rather her grandmother stirring a cup of tea.

"I didn't know you were here, Nan,"

"Hello Leah," her voice was seemingly stiffer than usual, although the mild scent of her perfume was always enough to dispel any tension.

"Are you making us dinner tonight?"

"I'm just here helping your father."

The screen door snapped open and Charles marched in as it swung shut. There was a definite negative sort of aura about him, yet Leah could tell this was a bit different to standard family squabbles. He ran his hand through his hair,

"Nowhere on the property, unless he's tucked away somewhere ignoring me calling for him,"

"What's going on?" asked Leah.

"Likely that's exactly what he's doing, he'll emerge when he's ready," said Ruth.

"No. No, this is strange, he always comes out if I tell him I'm serious,"

"What's going on?"

"Or he'll give away his hiding place being noisy or something,"

"He may have just wandered into the fields over the hill, he'll know his way back,"

"Dad, what's –"

"Leah, have you seen your brother?"

She flinched at the sudden attention and shook her head.

"You're sure?"

"I've been in my room all day,"

Charles grabbed his car keys and a sleek black brick that clipped to his pants (a 'mobile' phone – Leah wanted one),

"It's going to be dark soon," he said, "I'll have a drive around, maybe he's wandering on the roads or something. Mum can you stay here and call me if he comes home?"

Leah watched Ruth grab her son's shoulders and kiss him, "He will turn up, I know it. Try not to worry,"

"I can't lose another one,"

There was a look in her father's eyes that Leah had never seen before.

"Did Locky run away?"

Nan sipped her tea, "We're just not sure where he is, love,"

"He and Dad hate each other,"

"No Leah, they love one another; they're allowed to disagree though, both of them need to realise that,"

"They fight all the time now,"

"I'm sorry you're stuck in the middle of that, love; it's a dreadful spot to be in,"

"I never fix it, even though I try,"

"It's not your job the appease people, Leah – I mean that. It's misery the way people fight,"

Leah took a biscuit off Nan's plate.

"And you shouldn't stay in your room, either," Nan continued, "this is your house too and you don't have to walk on eggshells,"

"It's just easier sometimes,"

"I understand love, but you must let people know you won't be pushed around, that you won't have a bad day just because someone else dragged you down,"

"Aren't boys just like that?"

"No real man," said Nan, "your father's a good role model, but even grown-ups need to be reminded at times of what's right,"

The end of Leah's biscuit grew soggy in Nan's cup.

"They're sad because they miss Mum,"

"That's fair enough to be sad, but no excuse to snipe at one another. You make better progress when you connect with others; gather little pieces from one another to build each other up. You'll never have all the answers, but you can always freely remind your family that you love them,"

The phone rang;

"Let's hope that's news of Locky – hello?"

Leah gazed out at the twilight settling over the hills. The cicadas were out in force, drowning the evening scene with a tremulous symphony.

"Oh, Rebecca how are you?"

The neighbour's cattle dog barked in the distance, and Leah could hear a train whistle over the horizon.

"Lock? Where?"

Leah turned her head to Nan who stared intently at the floor.

"In Braidwood?! Oh, he is in trouble. You will? Thank you so much. I'd better call Charlie, he's out looking for him,"

She hung up the receiver.

"Your brother's gone and walked himself all the way to Braidwood."

In a storm cloud of teenage angst, Locky had walked some thirty-three kilometres across six or seven hours into town, where a neighbour had discovered him sulking in a park. With his imminent return, Ruth turned her attention to the evening ahead; it was too late to drive back to Goulburn; she'd stay the night with them. One look at the cupboards had her shaking her head as she and Leah decided on making dinner,

"That bloody father of yours," she hissed, "What's he feeding you lot? You need a grocery shop,"

"Sunday, usually," said Leah, "can we just have vegemite toast?"

Ruth laughed, "I think that sounds wonderful."

Charles arrived home first, still breathing anxiously in a cold sweat. Night had well and truly fallen by the time a new vehicle turned into the long driveway at the bottom of the hill, and Leah watched the pair of headlights weave up the drive knowing her brother was inside, uncertain how everyone would react to his homecoming. She listened from the screen doors at the call between neighbours, the 'thank you so much', the 'see you soon', the 'stay out of trouble', before a crumbling sound of tyres turning on the gravel, and her brother sheepishly walking into the dim light of the kitchen; time stood still for a moment amongst the four of them. Locky stared at the ground and sporadically glanced at his father and grandmother, as Charles pulled his son into a hug and sobbed into his shoulder,

You idiot, son; what did you think you were doing?

Do you realise how worried I was?

Jesus, boy; you are in so much strife.

Thank God you're safe.

Come on, Dad; it's not a big deal.

FIFTEEN

He wandered through other rooms, at another time – early morning; where he would usually rise late if given the option, Locrian had begun waking when the sun was young. A certain quality of dawn froze time, or gave an impression of reversing it; for he found himself in those newborn hours longing most for times past, thinking of people in their time and season, tearful of a day gone by. The bright and joyous sunlight did nothing to avert his gaze from it, if only he'd look forward, he might relish in the promise of a new day.

The other room, one he rarely perused – his father's bedroom – displayed an innocence of assumption, that its inhabitant would return at any moment. A pair of jeans folded over an armchair; a wrist watch laying on the bedside table; the doors of the closet hanging ajar as though they had been left in a rush. The bed had been hurriedly thrown together, given he wasn't one for visitors, his dad never felt the need to have the house looking too presentable – near enough was good enough. A dog-eared copy of Vonnegut sat on the night stand, bookmarked forever at page 134, bringing a wistful smile to Locrian's face – he'd mentioned the book to his father in the past; he'd clearly remembered and thought to read it for himself.

What's wrong, mate; what happened?

Scared of the thunder. I had a bad dream. Really bad.

Dreams can't hurt you, mate.

What if the lightning starts a fire?

I promise you it won't.

Can I sleep here?

Hop in, buddy.

Locrian sifted through the night stand drawers, momentarily forgetting what he searched for; where a person might keep their will had never been a question he'd considered until now. It would be best for him to leave it to Leah, but he wanted to be helpful and could think of no other way. He gave up on his search and moved to the window, where the morning frost lay thick on the panes.

"I thank God for another day,"

His phone buzzed in his pocket, a reply from Leah, although he'd forgotten he'd ever messaged her in the first place.

The house! You're right, it's exactly the same! Still a day away, sorry. Dealing with some stuff at home. See you tomorrow x.

The admission of delay came as a mild shock to his temperament, for he had expected this day to be a busy one, travelling to Queanbeyan to consult their father's solicitor, but now the slate had been wiped clean entirely. A tightness pressed his chest, a sensation of being trapped, of energy with no outlet; he gazed at his hand, lashed in uneven patterns by the thorns of weeds, and gazed at the half-eaten bag of peanut butter pretzels he'd sustained himself on for a day and a half – he would do well to move his body, if only to outrun his mind and remind himself of a physical prowess he still possessed in spite of the yoke of approaching middle age. He would run somewhere, anywhere; see old sights in the light of a new decade.

No matter the miles of experience in his legs, the outset of a long run often proved to be troublesome and usually left Locrian doubting of his ability to cover any sort of distance. This morning, however, the anxiety to begin was swiftly quashed, and in little time at all he felt the tingling of sweat overcoming the brisk air that engulfed the bushlands. The road to Captain's Flat was some ten miles from his childhood home (sixteen kilometres made more sense to him, but most of the running influencers he'd seen online were Americans speaking an imperial language) and given the day was his to do as he pleased, he thought to fill his hours with an absent productivity. To run such a distance was usually a panacea to the overactive mind, a meditation away from the darkness that shrouded him; that he might outpace the cobwebs that clung and sweat away the fever of unidentifiable dread that surrounded him. His flight on a flurry of aging feet carried him along, a hurrying through frostbite over the unpaved road that would stretch the first twelve kilometres of his pilgrimage.

Amongst a warbling of magpies he felt an opening of his heart, a valve released and a torrent of emotion, neither joy nor sorrow, race through the rivulets of his veins, for it was both a wonder to be alone and running on his two strong legs, and unbearable tragedy to pilot the remainder of his days without his patriarch. The song of the wild fluted its melodious bell-call past shrill beaks and mottled plume, as the piebald birds parted the grasses for progress in their wanderings. Long were the trails through the thicket, cloyed with wattle dressed as sun – little stars that bloomed among a vagabond sepia. For Locrian, a simpler rhythm of bone on rock, a pressure of puffed breaths forced by footfall from his being, there to hang in heated clouds about his mouth.

A sense of clarity settled him, an idea that there was no grief or sorrow, only a reaction to it; perhaps he could carry on, still feel happiness, remain the benefactor of simple pleasures. Life had led him here to this moment, sought to ferry him over every shoal thus far, so even the approaching sound of a vehicle would not throw off his rhythmic running. That is to say, the echoes of a spluttering engine could never drive a nail of anger through his madness; a drone of ascending volume, a shepherd's tone of irritation, louder and louder, concealed still by the trees and distance. No, he would not be swayed, he'd keep running, count his steps with increased difficulty, the mosquito whine of the speeding vehicle pounding louder in his skull. He turned his head to where the sound came from, seeing nothing but the prison bars of tree trunks, but knowing on this narrow road that he'd need to make way for the car to pass, that in turn it would have to acknowledge his existence as pedestrian. He cursed that bellow, the shattering of shale beneath his foot, for he could no longer focus on the ground before him. His anxiety cresting, heart racing; the offending vehicle roared passed him – an old Holden Ute travelling much too fast for the country road, sending Locky into the ferns, where he leapt for fear of being struck; the driver shouting some obscenity at him that he couldn't properly discern, before keeping its pace off into the distance in a cloud of dust. Rage overcame him – he pulled himself to his feet and threw a stone in the direction of the Ute that was far off ahead of him already.

"Moron!" he shouted, "Slow down! Idiot!"

Dust gathered on his sweat-covered forearms, the combination of physical exertion and primal fear had his chest pounding erratically; Locky slowed his pace to a walk and collected his bearings. His watch began to beep in a beat of warning to his elevated heart rate, 10.8km covered, not far until he reached the town, and soon he knew his path would change to a paved road where he could coast downhill into the valley. It was always *those* type of cars that were driven so unsafely; their drivers fulfilling their own stereotype. Locrian did his best to quench the anger that mounted inside him but all he could do was seethe. Death had overtaken him at 6.7 miles and snatched away with it the peace he'd so tenuously cultivated; try though he might, he couldn't regain that equilibrium.

Nobody visited Captain's Flat unless they had reason to be there. It gave no reason to stop or pass through, and unless one lived there it could go by unknown to all bar the most eager of cartographers. The once respectable mining town had been in decline for close to a century. So it was that any person who may have been out in the streets on that late morning might have found it puzzling to observe the running man who jogged into town like a crippled cowboy. There was a small park at the centre of the township, where Locrian sought to quench his thirst at a water fountain and plonk himself down onto a bench. In the stillness of the day the sun was bleak, held harshly overhead – interrogating, leaving few shadows for anyone to hide. And yet there was nothing to conceal, the daylight shone indifferently on the almost alien landscape of the mines, long closed; the pines that grew jagged from the ochre soil; the cars that stood silently on the streetside.

The pub was closed on Tuesdays, so said the sign, as Locrian poked his way about in search of respite, *feelin' bout half past dead,* and found no-one to confirm the town's lifeblood, instead left blind crying in the harsh sun and wishing to be heard. As his body cooled, the foreboding of true isolation draped over him in shivers; given that he'd need to conserve energy for the return run, he opted against climbing the hill of the old mine to survey the town and instead approached the petrol station with trepidation, as the windows of the general store were black and gave no indication of being open for business. The door opened though, revealing cramped shelves of groceries beneath a lazy ceiling fan. Still he saw no people, the ceiling fan belying the time-frozen canvas of a certain painterly quality, a movement in lull. Whatever he chose to purchase would need to be of a manageable size for him to run home with. He placed a bottle of water on the counter and was startled to see the shopkeeper had been sitting there the whole time, camouflaged against a display wall of cigarette packets.

"You're lost," he smirked.

"Huh?"

"You look lost," he repeated, "did you run here or something?"

"Yeah; sorry, you scared me,"

"Not much going on today; then some strange running man shows up in my shop,"

"Passing through,"

"Everyone is. You're not from here, I know that much,"

Locrian wasn't in any mood to talk, "I don't live here anymore. I used to live a few clicks towards Braidwood,"

"Used to, he says," said the shopkeeper, "Doesn't belong anymore."

Locrian left, bemused; hesitating to drink from the water bottle, fearing that strange man must have poisoned it somehow; he was compelled by an urge to leave, and leave immediately. Another sign thanked him for visiting Captain's Flat; his legs beginning to protest at the prospect of running again, the sun at its zenith, the trees towering over him – an insect that must scurry away from the swooping of birds. Although relieved to have left the ghost town in his wake, Locky found himself unable to reclaim the momentary joy he'd felt when he'd left the house, as though he'd exhausted any positive emotion he might have uncovered within himself. His feet dragged him across the tide of cicadas that screamed without end in the bushlands surrounding. Yet they should not have been making such a calamity of sound, Locrian had thought; the day had warmed considerably but it was unusual for those brash insects to be awake this time of year. An old sandstone church came into view – he had paid it no attention on the way over – and its presence in such isolation presently revived the detached dread of the town he'd just left behind.

Did I remember to thank God for another day?

The morning had dragged on forever, he could no longer recall if he'd muttered his mantra, despite the day having descending into a dour affair, and he concluded that he wasn't terribly thankful at all for it or how it had played out. Afternoon had crawled onto the property by the time he had arrived home.

SIXTEEN

September 2022

The revealer of new growth, the spring, often brought forth the good intention of positive change for those who dared to imagine. It had been mostly Lydia's idea to embrace it, as she decided the two of them must stop 'playing house' and take the at times awkward step of meeting one another's family. Locrian had ceded to her persuasion and made contact with his dad and sister, enough text messages to at least convince Lydia that he was making an effort. Perhaps to prove her point, Lydia decided they would take the long drive to visit her father as well.

Will he approve of the moody weasel who is dating his little girl?

Best limber up in case you have to run.

Good one. Good joke, right?

If humour had been her intent, it was deadpan beyond recognition. To be fair, her vivacity vanished in the week leading up to the visit, insomuch that their roles switched, and Locrian found himself appeasing her with a feigned light-heartedness that she saw right through.

You don't seem all that excited; is there a problem?

Not yet, at least. You never know what you might discover.

My mysterious little Venus.

Why are you calling me that?

There was the hope that the weekend would come and go and that their life might regain the fervent vigour of their early days, for they had been together for close to a year now and had settled somewhat into a routine that walked the precarious line of mundane. Neither could deny the appeal of such a bond though, where talk at last became easy, and the deeper secrets within them could be aired without fear of rejection or prosecution. However, this one sticking point was proving to be quite a thorn, and despite his unexplained evasion of his own relatives, Locky was beginning to think it might have been simpler on them both if they'd gone to *his* father's place first. Still, he drove; drove his car – God only knew where – past the outskirts of Sydney with her beside him in the passenger seat, off in her own reverie, sunglasses covering any sort of read he might gain of her mood, hair flicking in the wind as they flew down the highway.

Lydia had barely spoken all morning, beyond setting up GPS directions and agreeing to a takeaway coffee. Locky couldn't understand it; he knew though that he was growing weary of the negativity to the point where he fidgeted in his seat, desperately trying to spark conversation but realising it was usually her who led the way. They were silent as the car was noisy; the old engine straining in fifth gear, the wind slapping the sides of the car, the music issuing forth from the stereo. Their owl figurine stood on the dashboard, wedged so that the slant of the windscreen held it still, the colour of its lacquered body fading under constant exposure to sunlight. Locky reached over to poke its body and hoot playfully, with Lydia only giving a sympathetic smile in return.

"You're so quiet; what's wrong?"

"Nothing," she said, "what is this?"

"Iggy Pop. *The Idiot.* One of my favourites,"

"Yeah fine, but why do we have to listen to CDs? What year is this?"

"It's all the car has; I don't know, it's just how I've always done it,"

"We should have taken my car – is what I'd say if I had one,"

She hid her face behind a sip from her coffee cup.

"Are you going to tell me what's wrong, or not?"

"I just want to get this over with, ok?"

They were finally able to pass the semi-trailer that had slowed their progress for some time.

"It doesn't have to be awkward; what are your parents like? Tell me about them,"

Lydia wound her window up, sealing in a sudden quiet.

"Dad. Mum's not there,"

"You've never told me about that – beyond the fact that they aren't together,"

"It doesn't matter where she is," she snapped, "or what happened. She not there,"

"Sorry,"

It was too late to save the situation; he could feel her anger rising, "What about you? You don't talk about your mother either. And you still haven't messaged your dad,"

"I did! I told you that!"

"I think I just want to go home,"

"What? We're 200km outside of Sydney,"

"I said I want to go home. Turn the car around, turn the –"

"I-I can't do that here, we're on a highway,"

"– car around. Do it. I'll open this fucking door and jump out. Turn the car around,"

"Alright, alright, I'm doing it ok? I'm going to do it."

He could do little more but grant the request, however drastic it seemed. She'd never behaved like that before, not in front of him at least, and this new part of Lydia's personality left him stranded in an uncharted field where any step could set off a landmine. He ached from the hours of driving, now inadvertently doubled, and wished the ground would open up and swallow him, that he might crawl back into bed and forget how much of an ordeal this had become. He glanced over to her, knowing she was crying behind the sunglasses, unsure of whether he should say anything or keep quiet. The fuel gauge was approaching empty.

"I just can't do it today," she said softly, "I thought I could; I know I should; but I can't. I can't face it."

SEVENTEEN

January 1995

"I keep thinking that if I'd noticed how serious things were earlier, maybe I could have prevented it,"

"You've mentioned this in the past,"

"It keeps popping up in my head," said Charles, "such simple solutions that I can't apply. There's no second chance,"

Dr. Antony considered, "You've made a lot of progress over the years with this; you've said yourself that those questions weren't bothering you anymore,"

"I know, yet I just remain stuck here. I say that I've accepted what happened so I can give myself a kind of rev-up; thinking it might kick me into gear and move forward, but it doesn't work,"

"Hmm. Have I mentioned informal fallacies to you before?"

Charles shook his head.

"Excellent, then perhaps I can tell you about a line of thinking that I see you displaying, and perhaps give you some clarity. There is a type of fallacy, an argument, in Latin it's called *post hoc ergo proptor hoc* – after this, therefore because of this,"

"Righto," said Charles, "can we pretend I'm an idiot while you explain?"

The doctor laughed, "Put simply – because 'x' happened, 'y' then happened. If a rooster crows before the sun rises, does that mean the rooster caused the sun to rise?"

"No,"

"So then, what happened to Candace is not your fault."

Charles felt a familiar shift in his chest, like a kickstand being pulled out from under him, the sensation felt when one realises they're about to fall, and tears welled in his eyes once again.

"I've tried moving forward alone," he said, "but I struggle to deal. I have nobody to share the burden with,"

"I can understand that; that is what I'm here for,"

"I know, but I don't want to be stuck in therapy all my life either. Coming up to four years since it all happened, yet every time I might introduce myself to a woman, it all rushes back and there's just nothing there. Nothing but her,"

"Probably a sign that you aren't quite there yet. Perhaps you're looking to replace Candace rather than forge a new partnership,"

"I just want her back. I need her. I need companionship, but there's only her, and she's gone,"

Neither of them spoke for a moment.

"I can't," said Charles, "face this. Can't carry it alone. Yet I'm expected to hold it together in front of the kids. All I really want to do is scream and have someone hear me – notice that I'm not handling this. I wish she could hear me. See what she did to me, leaving me behind,"

"There will always be 'what ifs', especially when a person is gone from our lives. I know you loved your wife. Anybody who knows you can see that. You need to stop blaming yourself for what happened,"

Charles sat with his head in his hands. Dr. Antony waited.

"It just. It fucking haunts me, consumes my thoughts,"

"Memories can't hurt you. They can be distressing though. Maybe we can look at a shift in perspective; Ouroboros – does that word mean anything to you?"

Charles laughed wryly over his tears, "You're laying the philosophy on thick today,"

"Hopefully giving you confidence that I might help you – shall I continue?"

"Yep, go on,"

"Ouroboros is the snake who eats his own tail. It's an ancient symbol you might have seen or heard of before. But why do I bring it up? There is a duplicity of meaning behind it that can alter depending on your perspective. A creature who destroys himself, but consumes to give itself life. A death out of which new life is born. Cycles that repeat themselves; if you keep holding onto this blame, be unforgiving to yourself, you won't be able to move forward. When the time comes, you will be able to progress. Until then be aware of the moments when you find yourself repeating a negative line of thought. I see you shaking your head – you are capable of this, Charles,"

Exhausted of grief, Charles stared blankly at the bright window.

"If I use Latin words too, will I sound smarter? Or is that your fallacy again?"

"Ouroboros is Greek," the doctor smiled, "but I take your point."

EIGHTEEN

Tuesday, 12 August 2025

The shadows cast by the house lay in gloomy swathes across the hillside. Tall as their sins they stretched to the east, growing longer with time. From where they lay, they'd never touch heaven, exposed instead under the dying sun until they would vanish and merge with the horrors of night. A mortal man, a leader or patriarch, could build a fire that barely cut through the dark and present himself as a stumbling guide – the blind leading blind. Instead of lighting the way forward, those flames would bring close the monsters unbeknownst, where they lurked out of sight in memories somatic and suppressed.

Washed and dressed after his long run, Locrian sought calm enjoyment from his aching muscles, having accomplished something difficult; the woollen jumper that billowed comfortably over his frame, withholding the winter gale; the air that found purchase around his neck and cooled his blood-warmed head. His father's workshop stood atop the embankment nearest to the house, so that it might reign as sovereign overlooking the greater expanse of the property, and Locky approached this high place with a reverence he thought of as foolish. Verily the workshop expected no such praise; a rugged cobbling of timber and stone, windows had their glass shattered in jagged shards, leaving the roller shutter as the only means protecting its interior from the elements. It stood as a symbol of Charles Smith's duplicity of introvert and active father, embodying the qualities of a man with purpose found. Locrian had only recently come to the realisation that his father had reconciled his demons and brought peace upon his heart, but now that he was gone, the son remained lost ever more; the lighthouse had extinguished its beacon before Locrian's own shore-bound dawning, and now he felt more adrift than ever before. As such the workshop now appeared before him decrepit and cold. A series of brick-pit flowerbeds formed a small garden adjacent, the charred wooden beams above those beds suggesting it had once been a potting shed or greenhouse-like structure attached to the workshop, perhaps victim to a fire. To Locrian's memory, it had always been like this – he could remember no such potting shed ever being there. But the beams betrayed – black, rotten things propped up on skeleton columns of gnarled timber. The garden beds themselves were overrun with dried grass and the occasional dusky red bloom of a rose left to neglect.

He reefed open the shutter with more force than necessary, losing grip on the handle as it ascended, his own strength surprising him. To hear the thing clatter against the beam overhead he cringed; a pair of startled crows took off at the sound, and the smell of sawdust permeated the air. Pulling the switch, the light globe buzzed above him, giving colour and contour to the space left separated from the weakening afternoon light. Locrian smiled sadly to observe the half-finished projects and relics of his past strewn here and there; the workshop had that same fervent energy of his father's house, the musings of its busy inhabitant laid bare and vulnerable to the intrusion of the child unveiling a parent's personal world. *So he had been more than a vigil, more than a footnote* – it was funny to see a parent as more than that; that Locky's father was invariably just another man, a man who carried his own values close to his person, next to his troubles, and moved to guide his children through the perils of the lives playing out before them. And then, when the storms were calmed, the children happy, could he tinker towards his own personal interests. The more Locky saw, the more his regret increased – why hadn't he made the effort to visit more often? Five years had slipped through his grasp – he had only to reach out and grab at any opportunity, but he had not done it.

Amongst the clutter a crate of vinyl records leant against an old sound system – a boxy contraption of wires and dials that looked cobbled together for an all-in-one purpose – Charles had used the thing to death. The dials were grubby with finger grease, the speaker wires frayed.

If it ain't broke, don't fix it.

Locky reminisced on the afternoons filled with the noise of the sound system, tuned to whatever football match was on,

Thinking about the drop goal, here goes the shot… He has nailed it! He's got it, the halfback!

In later years the din had to combat with Leah's own CD player booming from upstairs in the house, when Locky would have given the world for a moment of quiet. Today that silence pervaded, whether he still wanted it or not. He flicked through the 33+1/3's, recoiling at his selfish thoughts of now claiming them for himself. There was some great stuff there – from The Doors' *Strange Days*, to Velvet Underground, even a tattered copy of The Beatles' *Sgt. Pepper*. It appeared as though his father had been working at repairing the needle arm that lay next to the turntable, each component placed carefully beside a notepad full of his neat, draftsman-like handwriting.

His eyes fell upon the framed Cronulla Sharks jersey on the wall.

See what I got?

It's cool, Dad. Shame it's the 2014 jersey.

Why's that?

We came last that year!

Must be why it was so cheap.

How cheap?

Free! Trust you to know what year it's from.

The sponsorship was a giveaway — or lack thereof.

I don't bother remembering all that stuff. You want a Sharks jersey? It's a Sharks jersey.

It was with great surprise that Locrian discovered his old guitar behind a wreckage of picture frames and boxes; stringless, so that the darkness of the sound hole stared out at him, the tuning pegs rusted so they could be turned no longer, a painted seagull on the body chipped and faded.

There's my C-major shape — Now what? I strum it; down, down, up, up, down, up.

Like the Konami code!

What the hell are you talking about?

Never mind, Dad.

Charles had made an effort to involve himself with the video games Locky played, but *Super Metroid* had been the only game he'd enjoyed – both of them had been shocked to discover that beneath heavy metal armor, the main protagonist Samus was a woman.

More fool us for assuming an armour-clad space warrior would have to be a man.

Locky had played so many games over the years, yet his father had been happy to replay the same old ones time and again. Their Super Nintendo system peered out from an open box, coated in a thick dust; Locky doubted it would still function.

Trust me, mate. The games are fun but don't neglect your music. You'll be an incredible guitarist in no time, I'm sure of it.

As a teenager it had been so easy to slip into the fantasy worlds offered in video games, and for a long time they'd been more important than honing his musical craft. It had only been the reaction of others that nudged Locky back towards a consistent music practice – turned out people were more impressed by musical prowess than being able to speed-run a thirty-year-old Nintendo game.

How could he bare to throw any of this away? Conversely, how could he ever hope to siphon through the piles of junk a person left behind? It occurred to him that he and Leah would soon need to pack it all up, decide the value of each individual item; was there any worth in holding onto old memories? Or was it better just to turn tail and continue forward? Maybe it was better to compartmentalise the mind, forget the physical objects, instead just file away the emotions of times past to a corner of the brain both accessible but set apart.

Sorting through the workbench would be straightforward in the least, as the tools that hung on the wall were rusty and useless, the shelves lined with little more than glass jars filled with nails and other pieces that *might be useful someday*. Charles had been working on a pyrographic wood-carving that he had perhaps intended to hang from the letterbox. The heat gun sat cold on the bench next to more scraps of paper conceiving various titles crossed out and scribbled;

Charlie's Place – too generic.

House of Smith – why so formal?

Lot's Lot – cute, Dad.

His father rarely used his full name of Charlot; he'd thought it sounded too feminine, and had instead been Charles to anybody who knew him. It was bizarre to see him use the other end of his name, almost sinister and unbelonging – a mirrored reality that never was.

Locrian mindlessly sorted through the wood cuttings before a primal recoiling had him stumble backwards. He lurched in horror as a hideous sound cut through the air, that of a writhing hiss, and the sudden emergence of a brown snake that had hidden itself among the rubble of wood. Locky thrashed terribly, crawling backwards towards the open door of the workshop, knocking over several boxes as the serpent continued to twitch in place on the bench. When he had been able to establish what he considered to be a safe distance, he stood and tried desperately to compose himself. The snake's movements had slowed, punctuated by an occasional spasm, and from his vantage point Locrian could see what had happened – in the confused chaos the creature had bitten its own tail. His heart raced – it was most unusual for a brown snake to be spotted this time of year, yet he cursed his carelessness for the momentary lapse in logic that had seen him rifling through such a predictable hiding spot for the thing. It was no longer moving; Locrian was unsure whether a snake could poison itself, but this one looked dead, or had just become very still, he didn't know – he dared not go closer to confirm. The approaching evening brought a chill that burned the exposed skin of his hands; he grabbed a length of timber and prodded the snake from a distance but it did not react. The kookaburras cackled in the gum trees that swayed in the frigid wind, the dried grasses of the flowerbeds shivered, and Locrian imagined the beams above the garden engulfed in the flames that had so clearly destroyed them some indeterminable number of years ago.

NINETEEN

During the night, he dreamed. He dreamed that he was running late to work. Now this was a dream that often recurred; a beast fed on unsurety and watered by an insecurity of being that he hadn't addressed. It was the easiest of his recurring dreams to decipher, and a single example of suppressed neurosis he could actually acknowledge and understand. The story might alter to specifically suit the state his life was in at the time, but the emotions it produced would always affect the waking hours of the following day. He might have found himself cautious around a person who had chastised his dream self, or he would find himself sitting a little straighter at his desk. More frequently, he simply checked the time incessantly to satisfy the reality that yes, everything was fine, he need not be so vigilant.

And so, the ceiling above his bed would shift as he'd stare deranged, as good as dead, observing the shadows that crept about his slumbering form, paralysed to any movement of his own. The numbers on the digital clock might glow brighter, give off an artificial daylight that he'd have to squint to read, although that certainly couldn't be the time – he'd only recently retired for the evening. A new day had begun without him, already mature and functional, indignant to the disorganised man who tried to graft himself onto its industry.

Did you think you could just slip in unnoticed? The world won't wait for slouches, boy.

I'm sorry, my phone stopped working.

We left you three messages.

That's what they'd say at least. It was probably best to call in sick, take the day – a mental health day, God knew that no number of sick days could salvage *that* mind. Therefore, he would throw on a work-shirt, unironed and unwashed, and race out of the flat without breakfast or his keys – and thankfully the bathroom window was open and he could enter his home and retrieve said keys, although he really shouldn't be climbing the roof without a harness. Did he not realise how dangerous that was? Not to mention the grime left on his pants after clambering through an old window; now if he'd taken the time to dust and wipe down his home, that wouldn't have been a problem. Then came the issue of where he'd parked his car – it had to be in the house somewhere, yet how could it fit out the front door? Maybe he'd have to settle for walking to work, but by now it was mid-morning and it was probably best to call in sick. They'd all be in a meeting, chortling away;

Where's that Smith with a 'y'?

Who-with-a-who? Ah, him. What does he do again?

Yes, Mr. Client, yes. We've missed our deadline; our big up-and-comer called in sick — yes, yes, today of all days!

He was sweating right through his shirt — the business attire was ill-suited to physical exertion and it was a hot day. *Hot one out there today, pal — take care.* Feet weren't known to combust, but his just might, and he was thirty-three and a half kilometres away from the office. Could he shower at work? Freshen up? No, too much of the day was already wasted. The traffic was tremendous and the trains were cancelled and the footpaths were closed for construction.

You can't walk there.

Terribly sorry, I'll get out of your way.

It's fine, but you don't work here anymore, remember? What are you doing here?

You can trust me to stay quiet and out of the way, I won't even bother a soul.

Well, they *supposed* he could sit there if he really wanted to, they had no work for him to do though. Shouldn't he let his boss know that he's quit and gone back to his old job? It was past midday, probably best to call in sick.

You're back.

They let me sit here.

Why though?

She said.

Mumma said?

To get things done, I'd better not mess with Major Tom.

The sun hadn't risen yet but the glow of red lines across his bed came from the gaps in the blinds. Was there a fire next door? Couldn't be, just a swimming pool. He hated fire, that's how she – but no it isn't the luminance of flame; it's dust. Red dust all the way from the centre of the country, blown across the miles to his dank flat on this idle Wednesday. But that had happened once, hadn't it? Red dust storm one Sydney morning, God how his clothes had smelt terrible. Get out of bed!

I can't be back here again.

But you are.

I'm so late for work.

You don't have a job.

Probably best to call in sick.

The wife gave him a look of utter disappointment; God looked at him with disgrace. *You don't have a wife; how can you be sure God even knows you exist?* It was another day, a new chance to make things right. Turning up to work naked was a bold choice though, and the hat didn't suit. Everyone was looking at him; this was not the fashion statement he'd assumed it to be. But he was so far from home, too late now to go back and change into a proper outfit. She was dangling his keys over his head, and good Lord she was enormous. Her trunk was thick; her roots ran deep.

Oh, you want these, big boy? Can't get to work without them.

You need to stop this at once, my wife would never approve.

You don't have a wife.

My God would never approve.

Sounds like a prude.

Then he began to run, outrun those problems, elude the pursuit of that nameless mystery, but maybe he'd be better to relent, call in sick, enjoy the faded memory of pre-birth bliss regained upon death – but who wants to die?

I'm still here.

Leave me alone.

Face me and face yourself.

Put a Lyd on it.

You don't go to school anymore.

Yet she still had his keys, and he'd never get to work on time without them, it was probably best to call in sick. When had she gotten so massive? He struggled against her gravity. The keys left her hand in a powerful throw, whizzing through the air and into the swamp. He dashed down into the dank of the mangroves and waded gingerly into the shallows. *Hoist up those pants, boy*; too late, there's mud all over them. God, he shouldn't be here – he was supposed to be at work!

I got that watch for my birthday.

Keys.

And you've just gone and chucked it away.

You don't need the time, it's too late already.

I've ruined my pants.

Aren't you a little old for nocturnal emissions? How embarrassing.

The spasm pulsed through his groin, he hated that he enjoyed it. The cold had increased tenfold, showering a powdered snow atop his head in slow drifts. Soon he'd be snowed under, locked forever with that cold, damp patch on his pants disturbing a blizzard of fitful sleep.

TWENTY

February 2023

Across those summer months, he began to notice the presence of a shadow. It arrived without ceremony, and seemingly demanded no direct attention, lurking within the narrow confines of his peripheral vision or hanging above the blind spot behind his head. The nameless thing gave no impetus for its arrival, and there remained a thought in his head that this dissonant beast had always been there – he'd only now just given it credence. If he hadn't been preoccupied with a turn in Lydia's moods, he might have been able to confront the shadow, but as it were, he chose a route of further suppression, ignoring the deep-seated problem it might represent.

Lydia had not been the same since their failed attempt to visit her family. A certain negativity pervaded her effervescing persona and left Locrian with an urge to make things better for her. It was true that she made efforts to connect with him on the matter; state that it wasn't his fault, that she'd come around eventually, yet the only certainty that arose from the ordeal was that a second attempt was not on the cards. Locrian, frightened to test the subject, turned further within himself and ignored the calls and messages he would receive from Leah and his father. Were he to acknowledge that those messages were diminishing in number, he could have seen the true depths of the depression he waded in; especially from the contact of his father, whose tone and affliction had become hurried and incomprehensible, as though his son was no longer worth the effort. Or worse still, that he would give up trying after Locrian repeatedly declined incoming phone calls. His sister on the other hand, seemed busy with her own lot, and the valley of Locky's self-pity saw it fit to leave her be and not add his own troubles to Leah's.

"You never told me you had a niece," Lydia had said.

"I met her once when she was born, she'd be four or five now,"

"You should probably know how old she is, Lock,"

"All the more reason why I shouldn't be a parent myself,"

"Do you see children in our future?"

Her candour surprised him.

"We both know that's not possible," he said after a moment's thought, "my head isn't right. It would be selfish of me to bring another human into the world,"

Lydia appeared saddened yet resigned, and promptly began to bury herself in her art, filling several sketchbooks with the most intricate pencil drawings – many of which portrayed confronting subject matter that Locrian honestly didn't enjoy looking at.

"I guess there's a darkness inside," she said, "that needs an outlet. I don't expect you or anyone to look at these, really. You wouldn't go through someone else's diary, would you?"

"No, I suppose not. But you should tell me if there's something troubling you. I might even be able to help,"

They both laughed sardonically.

For Locrian, he dove headlong into composing music, writing pieces that might compliment the sharp-edged misery of Lydia's artworks. And yet he wouldn't play the music he wrote, rather seeing it in its corporeal form of ink on staff lines; to strike a key or pluck a string might send its mystique careening off into the aether, like a ripple from a stone dropped in water, further away from what it was meant to mean with each vibration that pushed it along a sonic tide.

"Well that makes sense," said Lydia, "that I can't hear your songs and you can't see my drawings,"

"I can't swim your waters," he mused, "and you can't walk my lands,"

"Tim Buckley,"

"Yep,"

"It's moments like this that remind me why I'm here with you,"

"You understand me; even the weird parts,"

Her smile was like a light.

Still the shadow remained cast, and when Locrian tried to fix his gaze upon it, the image would shift in a sort of quantum convulsion, unobservable and just barely outside his range of vision. Were he to catch sight of its face, he thought he saw his own grinning back at him with a malicious rictus, and he'd shake his head and squeeze his eyes shut and inwardly groan for the beast to just go – *go away*. He obsessed over his creations – *Pygmalion* – each composition carrying the full weight of his attention until it was given a final florid adornment and cast aside for the next project. A dam wall of artistry had burst and he could do little but tap the vein until it expired.

"God, this is pages of music," Lydia said.

"I don't think any of it is any good,"

"I can't comprehend it unless it's played,"

"Lots of musicians don't go to these lengths to scribe everything like this, it's probably senseless,"

"Hey, it's yours; like my drawings, perhaps they're just for you to hear in your head,"

"Jesus, Lyd – there's too much going on in my head already. I can't seem to quell it,"

"You're an artist, my love," she wrapped her arms around his chest, "the worst thing you've ever created was the last thing you made. The greatest work of your life is what you're currently working on."

He regrouped his love for her into a withering burst of devotion, determined to remind her of the intricate value she gave his life. Weeks could go by without Lydia showing any sign of distress or misery, yet he'd pursue meticulous lengths to ensure her happiness, pour his energy into servitude, give her the divinity of the queen he saw her as. She would smile and look away, embarrassed at the attention – not for herself, but rather that Locrian could behave in such a ludicrous manner just to impress her.

"Sometimes I wonder if my entire life is just a dream,"

"Oh shut up, you sap," she laughed.

"It's true," he continued, "but then I think, no – my mind can't conjure a love like yours,"

"Ass!" she threw a couch cushion at him.

That she loved him filled Locrian with confidence, had him consider that he could navigate the shoals of his mind's low tide and not run aground.

"Do you think I should spell it as 'Locke' instead? Like, with an 'e' at the end?"

"Spell it however you like, it doesn't make a difference,"

"Well maybe I'll just change my name entirely. Something really dumb, so you have to humiliate yourself every time you introduce me to someone,"

"Whatever, Mr. Flat-Five,"

"Wow, that's an old one,"

"Did you think I'd forgotten?"

Forgotten; the word carried weight. Could anything be forgotten? Better to ask if anything was ever truly gone. His mind would drift – was there ever a drought? All the water that ever existed was somewhere on the planet, maybe as ocean, maybe vapour, but never *gone*. He'd consider the dust that moulded itself into the shape of the woman he loved – that one day it would fall apart and return to the earth – still *her*, but just somewhere else. Her as ash, scattered to the winds – he shivered and held her tighter while they slept. But she was still awake.

"What's your earliest memory?"

"I don't know,"

"Sure you do,"

"I really don't think it matters,"

"Are you sure about that?"

"Memories of childhood are just so hazy – who can trust them?"

"What creates that haze? Is it a distance of time, or rather our inability to form proper thoughts at such a young age?"

"Can it be both?"

"Or neither,"

"I really don't want to talk about it. Ask me something else."

Time or ability or both. Locrian peeled back the curtain of his grandmother's passing, how dementia had ravaged her once strong mind. Still there, but this time gone – truly gone.

Don't cry, Lock; grandmothers are a child's gift. You're not meant to keep it for too long.

It just hurts. Losing anyone hurts.

You were an adult when she died – not everyone gets that.

Yeah but I was three when –

Shh, don't cry. It's late, let yourself drift off to sleep.

When his grandmother died, Locky's father had vehemently scorned the ailments of a failing mind.

"God, son," he said behind his tears, "I hope I never have to suffer like that. It was so hard to see her lose her mind; I wouldn't wish that on anybody."

Locky had held his father's shoulder, thinking about the sweet equilibrium of years between youth and old age when the brain functioned the way it was meant to, and how it was wedged between a darkness born of nothing – *ex nihilo* – and the gloom-soaked umbra of death that bookended life.

TWENTY-ONE

March 1999

The bell rang, cutting savagely through the hazy summer migraine. The cicadas mounted their case for chaos with an uproar that threatened to combust and set the bushlands alight. The strange sound of a school bell just might have been the flint strike to ignite a late summer day that was ready to burst. The school itself looked rudely intrusive against the eucalyptus trees that surrounded it; situated so defiantly in a place where nature claimed rule, it stood against the bushlands with the same threat of oppression often felt by the renegade students. It bristled in the aching heat, fibreglass walls contracting from the harsh season that gripped them, the shimmer of fata morgana weeping from the tin roofs of the demountable classrooms.

On that afternoon, when the sun was at its hottest, the grounds stank of foetid apathy; of teachers whose passion had turned perfunctory, of students who groaned with the awkward pains of growth. Nothing knew its place, and anything that claimed otherwise writhed in a nomadic denial. The shadows that hid themselves from the sun sapped the energy of the hours while all else lay distracted by the blind brightness, and discomfort swam in the awful headache of the day. When it seemed that no malady could sweat out that fever, the children broke out from their classrooms and ran for the bindii-covered field to proclaim their temporary freedom.

"It's Aussie rules," a child called, "half field, each year to themselves,"

"How's that fair? You seniors will pick on the kindy kids,"

Another child belted the bladder of the old Sherrin, so decrepit had it become, any lunchtime game could be its last.

"That's a major!"

"Bullshit! Hit the post, a behind,"

"You swore, I'm telling,"

"Fuck off."

Using only half the field for the game meant that the kids had less space – an advantage in the hot day where preserving energy went a long way towards staving off dehydration. It also meant that those with no interest in footy could sit and play on the other side, where there were less prickly weeds. Leah sat with her friends and watched the game play out, thinking about how stupid it all was.

Get knocked off your feet once and you'll be picking bindii weeds out of your clothes all day.

It was the kind of thing Nanna would say, and she took great lengths to try and emulate the way her grandmother spoke, otherwise they'd just call her a dumb little kid. Being the youngest was difficult, but at least Nan stood as a woman she could aspire to be. Her brother played footy, an act that surprised her, for he was always the shy kid who struggled to get involved in any kind of rough play.

He's having a crack, good on him.

Nan often said that, too.

The ball bounced away from the pack towards her and she indignantly batted the thing away with her fist.

"Gross, get it away,"

The others paid her no mind, and recovered the stray ball back to the cluster of bodies at the other end of the field. Locky occasionally found the ball in his grasp, running and bouncing it before producing an absolute shank of a kick that split the front of goal and bounced to the next child.

"Swannies win, Pies in the bin!" cried another kid.

"Boo, go Saints,"

"St. Kilda? Are you serious? They suck!"

"You suck."

They all sucked if you asked Leah. Sometimes you won, other times they lost. It seemed like an even split to her, and there was no point getting worked up about either result. The kids all had their team and would go blue in the face arguing why they were superior to another. Leah did like the colours, each team having their own jersey and moniker; there was no turtle team though, which she saw as a missed opportunity. She would also admit to being excited for the upcoming Olympic Games.

Presently she became aware of a rising tension amongst the group, maybe a hand pass would be a little rougher than it needed to be, or maybe a child would showboat a little too much after kicking a goal. She looked at her pink wrist watch and deciphered the hands (she'd taken great pride learning to read analogue). A couple more minutes until lunch ended, probably for the best – everyone was getting mean. Locky got the ball again and this time send a pearler of a kick straight between the sticks, where he cheered for himself with his few friends while others didn't look so happy about it.

"That was a fluke, dude,"

"Calm down Smithy, it was a good kick,"

"Fluke. If I played properly, Locky would be last every time. Stone motherless last,"

Smithy could see that his taunt had affected Locky.

"What a shame we have the same last name. You're a joke,"

"Shut up," Locky timidly replied.

Smithy's mates seemed split, some tried to calm him down while others egged him on,

"He *is* motherless last. He's a bastard,"

Smithy laughed, "A motherless bastard! Ha!"

"Bastard means no dad, though,"

"Does it? Who cares? It's totally true,"

Leah watched in horror as the older boys tore her brother apart with their words. She wished she could grow to their size and beat them up, but could only watch helplessly as Locky fought back tears.

"He's going to cry,"

"Cry to mummy?"

"He can't!"

"I heard she killed herself,"

"Probably took one look at his ugly mug and did it —"

A loud thud sounded as Smithy fell to the ground clutching his face. Locky fell with him and began wildly throwing his fists into him. Leah finally overcame her freeze and raced over to pull her brother away. Smithy's face was smeared red, a gash above his eye streaming blood across the sweat and dirt. It was now his turn to cry as he sobbed loudly in pain.

"Jesus, Locky," said one of Smithy's friends, "the fuck is wrong with you?"

Leah tried to hold Locky's hand but he wouldn't look at her, instead standing with fists clenched and chest panting.

"We were just messing around, dude. Now look what's happened. Don't you see this is all your fault?"

Leah tugged her brother's arm, desperately trying to lead him away from the conflict, and only when he finally turned and looked into his sister's eyes did he breakdown completely and weep openly, slowly shuffling his way back to the classroom as the bell rang again.

TWENTY-TWO

Wednesday, 13 August 2025

On the third morning, it snowed. Locrian awoke to the frigid morning with his pants damp, having come in his sleep. His skin was clammy under the heavy blankets, and the combination of the keys in his pocket and the stiff corners of the sofa made him writhe with discomfort. Outside the house, the fragile beauty of the winter scene presented itself chaste and pristine, and he left the window open as he showered and watched the steam float in clouds into the cold air.

"I thank God for another day,"

And perhaps he meant it today, such was the glory of the quiet snow drifts. He knew the rarity of this situation, that winters here could go by for years without snowfall, and never more than a handful of days any given year. Moreover, that the snow would likely melt away by midday and the brown grasses, the birds and animals would carry on as though it had never existed. The dam lay covered with a sludgy skimming of ice, and a pair of galahs huddled grimly under the cover of bottlebrush branches.

The coffee was made slowly before he surveyed the flurried hillside and considered the impending arrival of his sister – for today was the day – and how they might react to seeing one another again. There would no doubt be a tension seeping through the sadness, as he knew he'd been neglectful in contacting her of late. Yet maybe the grounding reality of their father's death would level the playing field somewhat, and he could lie to her and himself with little pleasantries;

Yes, I'm well.

I know, it's been too long.

This must be as hard for you as it is for me.

Foolish though, that he would feel the need to withhold candidness from his younger sister; their bond had been one built strong over the years, and he was not so delusional to hope they might slip easily back into the comfortable palaver they'd always had.

A kookaburra hopped about on the front lawn, scouring the snow layer for any insects that might be foolish enough to emerge, although it seemed the bird was having limited luck. Locky gave his legs a gentle stretch, aching from his run the day before, and warmed his injured hand on the coffee cup. In the driveway, his car sat gripped with frost, and eventually the sun emerged from behind the cloud cover and began to fight back the icy clutches of the night's storm.

A car pulled into the driveway at the bottom of the hill, and Locky watched in anticipation as it wound itself up the path and came to a stop in the mud outside the house. A taxi; its nameless driver retrieving a suitcase from the trunk and Leah tapping her phone on the machine to pay the fare. She was taller than he'd remembered, her face expressing a weary wisdom; in his mind she was still his kid sister, and he often forgot that they'd both become adults and changed from the memories he held in his head. She appeared frustrated; the driver had carelessly placed her bag directly on the wet ground, and Locky instinctively ran to her and grabbed the handle to bring it to the veranda.

"Hello stranger," her familiar voice brought a smile to his face.

"Hey,"

They held one another in a long embrace truncated by several pats on the back.

"How are you?" Locky asked, "Dumb question, I know,"

"Fine. I'm fine. Let's get inside, it's bloody freezing,"

"You missed the snow,"

He poured her a coffee as she adjusted her scarf, rubbing her hands together,

"The only fun part about the cold? Sounds about right. Jesus, it's so cold in here. Why haven't you got the fireplace going?"

Locrian paused briefly then continued stirring the fresh coffee.

"You should've called," he said, "I'd have come to the airport to get you,"

Leah sighed through her teeth, "I did, Lock. Called you twice, you didn't answer,"

He grabbed his phone from his pocket and tapped the screen – *Leah: missed call (3)* – he had not noticed.

"Reception's pretty bad here. You know how it is," he shoved the phone sheepishly back into his pocket.

"Mmhmm," she didn't push the matter any further, "God, the house has barely changed,"

She took a small turn about the living room, running her hand over surfaces and stopping in front of a side table with their picture on it.

"Seems smaller when you're an adult,"

"I said the same thing,"

"Talking to yourself again, bro?" she replaced the picture frame.

"As always. How is scenic Adelaide?"

Leah stopped to consider her words, "Comfortably terrible. You know, Georgia is six this year,"

"Hard to believe. Look, before you say it, I know I should have come over to visit at least once –"

"In the last five years? Yeah, you should have,"

"I'm sorry,"

"Don't worry about it," she replied, "nothing like a death in the family to bring us back together,"

She pulled up a stool at the kitchen bench. Locky leaned against the opposite side, holding his coffee cup in front of him like some pathetic little shield.

"I've been a bit caught up in my own head lately," he said, "but we're together now; can we try again?"

Leah shrugged; her smile was loving, yet a resigned sadness remained plainly evident.

The sun continued to break through the cloud cover intermittently, and the ground outside reflected its rays off the melted slurry on the ground. By now the snow had completely turned to water.

"So, Dad's gone," she finally said.

"Yeah," he paused before continuing, "I saw him the other day. We need to get his will and all that,"

"We'll get to that; geez they hurry you along, don't they? Not a minute to stop and grieve or even realise what's happened,"

He took her empty cup and rinsed it in the sink.

"What happened to your hand?" she asked.

Locky looked to the cuts on his palm, "Oh, lantana. The other day. Slipped and grabbed at a weed and here's the result,"

Leah sucked her teeth, "Ouch. No guitar playing for you,"

"I don't really play anymore. Not since I burnt my hands,"

"You burnt your hands?"

"No, forget it. Not sure what I'm talking about," he waved his hand dismissively.

"Alright then," Leah rolled her eyes and stood, "I'm going to go check out my old bedroom,"

"If you can get in there, go for it. You'll see what I mean,"

The old stairs groaned beneath her feet.

"Lee," he called; he had a sudden urge to mention the gravestone he'd found at the back of the property, but then decided against it, "Careful up there. I saw a snake in the shed yesterday."

Left alone again momentarily, he became assailed by the versions of himself that he had sculpted during the time spent apart from his family; self-conscious of the man he had become since he'd last seen his sister, who alongside him was the last remaining of his bloodline – the blood he knew at least – and that he was truly unmoored now. There was no cavalry to come and rescue him from the torture he inflicted upon himself, just his younger sister, who he felt should not be burdened by the torments of her older kin. What had he become, and what did he have left to give, keep or gain? Leah's arrival had shifted a capstone in his reality – it was easy to lie to oneself in solitude; *burnt his hands* – why had he said that? The lie had come so easily. It was a small thing to dwell on, but he knew the domino effect of pathological falsities.

"Wow, Dad became a bit of a hoarder at the end there, didn't he?"

Leah stomped back down the stairs and broke his train of thought before it fully derailed itself. It took Locrian a moment to correct himself.

"By himself, I guess. He just shoved everything else in a corner, in those old rooms,"

"He could have kept our rooms how we remembered them," said Leah, "but I guess it's his house. We moved out, he can do what he likes,"

"Things hidden away,"

"What's that?"

"Huh? Nothing,"

Again, she gave him that questioning look.

"Well anyway, I need to do something about the heating situation here,"

The fireplace was at least clean of ash and soot, their father had upkept those few rooms in the house that remained in use; wood was stacked neatly to the side of the firebox. Leah placed kindling inside and built a small pyre before standing and looking around.

"Got a lighter?"

Locky was standing in the kitchen with his eyes shut tightly.

"Sorry what?"

"Or matches? I'll get it going and warm the place up,"

He opened the top drawer and found a matchbook. Reaching out for his hand, Leah's sleeve slipped, and something there caught her brother's attention.

"Hold up," he said.

Leah tugged the sleeve back down and quickly moved back to the fireplace.

"Reckon I still remember how to do this," she laughed nervously.

"I said wait. What's that on your wrist?"

Realising there was little point in concealing, Leah presented her forearm, which was covered in deep, purple bruising.

"I fell," she said, "in my backyard. Hurt my arm, not broken or anything, ha. Looks like we're both having silly accidents,"

Despite being aware of how contradictory he was about to sound, Locrian spoke firmly, "Are you lying? Did someone do this to you?"

Leah struck a match, but it broke and fell to floor. She struck another, which burned for a few seconds before extinguishing. She dropped the entire matchbook and put her face in her hands; when he saw her eyes again, they were welling with tears.

"Ok, you got me," she said softly, "things haven't been great at home,"

Locky was aghast, "*He* did this?"

Leah stared out the window and nodded erratically, wiping her eyes clear.

"Leah, why didn't you tell me? And Georgia, she's —"

"With her father, yes. He'd never do it to her, I know that,"

"Fuck, you're sure?"

"Yes, Lachlan. And I'm not here to talk about this, ok? Let's just get Dad's stuff sorted and get out of here."

She knelt down to light the fire while Locky compulsively shook his head in disbelief. He wanted to comfort her, fix her problems, but could do nothing but stand there uselessly. Guilt came roaring back from deep within; he thought of all the times Leah had messaged him, left him calls that were unanswered; he thought of how *Lydia* had repeatedly insisted that he reach out to his sister. Paralysed with indecision, and caught in a riptide of overlapping emotion, he grasped for the right words to say to her but came up empty.

"Leah," he said, "how long?"

With the fire lit, she stood and angrily threw the matchbook into the flames where it combusted in a bright and momentary spark.

"What does it matter, 'how long'? You'd bloody know if you made the effort to talk to me. How long, how long – fuck off! How long did I wait for you to answer your damn phone? To reply to a message?"

Her fury was reaching a peak.

"And what about Dad?" she continued, "he was sick and needed us. We let him down. I couldn't get over here because of *him*. You needed to stand up be here, but you weren't. Dad died alone,"

"I – I didn't realise he was sick," he stammered.

"Yeah, well good lot of use that news is to you now,"

She stood with her arms akimbo, the way she used to when she was a child.

Her voice dropped low, "Just – where were you?"

He hated the tears that had begun to form in his own eyes, "I can say sorry and truly mean it. Truly mean it, I'm sorry, Leah. But they're just two words and it doesn't fix anything,"

They were interrupted by a knocking at the door.

TWENTY-THREE

April 1996

"I gave up a lot of her possessions last weekend,"

"I can imagine that was a difficult thing to do,"

Charles scratched at the dog Mitzi's ear, "Yeah, I guess I thought it was time,"

"Tell me more about it,"

"I still had all her clothing hung up in the wardrobe. Her books, her makeup – God some of that stuff had gone bad, let me tell you,"

"And did you have any process to it all?"

He thought for a moment, "Yes and no, I guess. I'd deliberated on it for a long time; what I'd keep, what I'd get rid of. I suppose when it came time to actually doing it, it was pretty methodical,"

The sound of Dr. Antony's pen scratching against his notebook filled the room.

"There's the guilt," said Charles, "about moving forward. I know it needs to happen, but I can't help but think I'm leaving her behind,"

"It's a fairly common trait that we would tie a person's value up in their possessions,"

"Mum had an interesting thought; that if I gave all those clothes to St. Vinnie's, they'd get a new life. It made me feel better about it all, that I wasn't just chucking it away to landfill,"

"Were the kids aware of what you were doing?" the doctor asked.

"Leah helped. She was stoked, to be honest. Five-year-olds just like to help; be kept busy, feel useful, you know?"

Dr. Antony laughed, "I understand that,"

"It gave me a chance to give her some of the more special items that belonged to her mother. A bit of jewellery and the like,"

"I'm sure she'll treasure those things,"

"Yeah. Lock though, didn't want a bar of it. He doesn't speak much about his mum; I try to give him that space, but I don't know," he trailed off.

"He's still young," the doctor replied, "just keep offering that support,"

"I worry that he lacks empathy. He's a sweet kid, mostly. Yet I can't get him onboard with a lot of things. I worry that I'm not doing a good enough job making him a decent human being,"

Dr. Antony paused, "I wouldn't go so far to be concerned about a lack of empathy. Children his age are still very inward-focussed, and he's been through a lot. Has he got hobbies? Things he shows interest in?"

"He loves music," Charles face lit up, "dead-set talent, my boy. We got him into guitar at school, and his grandmother's piano is finally getting some use – she reckons we should just take it from her,"

"That's fantastic,"

"I've just got to try and encourage his gift. I don't know shit about music other than listening to it,"

"You can get him to teach you a thing or two," the doctor suggested, "a way you might get involved, validate his interest, show you care,"

Charles was nodding, the thought hadn't crossed his mind before. He knew one or two chords on a guitar, but that was it.

"I just don't want him to think," he said, "sorry just dialling it back here – that I was removing his mum from our lives by sorting through her things,"

"Well, you keep the important things; the memories, the photographs,"

"There's little things you kind of forget though. Her smell, God, it was still on her clothes. It made sorting through it tougher,"

"That's what we call a somatic memory. Something felt by the body, the senses. They can be underlying and tricky to spot, but play a big role in how we can feel about certain things,"

"Do you think my son might experience this?"

"Absolutely, we all do. It's simply a function of our body, a way of remembering different things. If the sensation is tied to a traumatic event, then it can be unpleasant, but it's a survival mechanism,"

Charles shifted uncomfortably, "Like a fear of fire?"

Dr. Antony held the space for a moment, "Yes, I suppose. One might associate the smell of smoke with their stress responses, for example,"

Charles closed his eyes, his breaths coming to him long and purposefully. The doctor waited.

"It's been five years this month," said Charles, "every time I think I've turned a corner, some intrusive thought comes knocking and just, just rattles me,"

"And you're doing very well. Remember your progress. It's been said that we have a certain number of stress responses in trying situations – you've heard of fight, flight, etcetera?"

Charles nodded.

"So that's our response *in* the moment. But what do we do when memories of a traumatic event come back at a later time? I like to look at three modes here; repress, relive, recall. We can squash those thoughts down, try to forget them, ignore to avoid discomfort – that's repression. Then we have relive – we can find ourselves back in the moment, and that can trigger things like panic attacks and the like – not good. It's that third option – recall. That's the one we should aim for. We don't want to forget the bad things that happen to us; they build us, refine us. But we don't want to relive them either; that restrains us, holds us back from moving forward. Now recollection – well that's like any other memory. We can recall, turn it over in our head, acknowledge it as a part of us, and move on. That's what we want to aim for."

TWENTY-FOUR

Wednesday, 13 August 2025

From where they stood, they could see the shadows of feet beneath the back door in the mudroom, and the through the fogged glass panels, the presence of two humanoid shapes broke the isolated battle of Leah and Locrian's argument. Neither brother or sister spoke, both of them grappled with the sensations of sibling squabbles from a time long past, when their dad would enter the scene to put an end to the commotion.

I don't care who started it, we're finishing it now.

Gaining her composure a moment before her brother, Leah gestured to the door with a sweep of her arm,

Go on then, care to open it?

Locky hurriedly entered the mudroom and opened the door, where an elderly couple had begun to turn away and walk back to the unknown car that had discreetly arrived on the property. When they turned to the sound of the opening door, their faces softened, and Locky was certain he recognised them. A cattle dog tugged at the leash held by the old man, its tail wagging erratically.

"Oh, apologies, we assumed nobody was home," the woman said, no doubt a lie – the entire valley had probably heard Locky and Leah fighting.

"Jacob," the woman called to the man who Locky assumed was her husband, "Jacob, they're home,"

"Ay?"

"I said the kids are home, look,"

Locrian held the door, once more tied of the tongue, and said nothing to dispel the awkward tension. Behind him, Leah had appeared and took control of the pleasantries,

"You live down the road, don't you?"

The woman smiled, joyful at the recognition, "Yes, that's right. You remember us, Leah and, and –" she clicked her fingers, "Lachlan, wasn't it?"

"Locky is fine,"

"Sarah and Jacob," said Leah.

Locky was relieved that his sister knew who they were; he could see their faces, clutch at a strand of recognition, yet had been unable to place them. He cycled through a maelstrom of faces in his mind –

yes, there they were; his neighbours from the next property over, he had not thought of them in years.

"Come in," ushered Leah.

Though he was hopeless with idle chatter, Locky knew that he could make himself useful and brew some more coffee, and as he collected a set of cups, he hoped that the gesture of hospitality might pay to his repentance to Leah, who spoke freely and easily – unshackled from the chains her family life had strapped to her.

"You're both so grown up," Jacob was saying, "last time I saw you lot, you'd have been teenagers,"

Leah scratched at the dog's ears with both hands, the beast fidgeting about for the attention she gleefully gave.

"It's a shame we see you again under the circumstances," said Sarah.

"I suppose we knew this was coming for at least a few months," Leah replied, giving her brother a bitter glance, "still a shock for it to happen though,"

Locky emptied a packet of biscuits for them onto a plate and sat down.

"We're dreadfully sorry about Charlie," said Sarah, "he wasn't all that old either. I hope you know we did what we could for him,"

"Yes," added Jacob, "Sarah here dropped by every day to check in, but it got to a point where we had to organise a house nurse,"

Silently sipping his black coffee, Locky listened without speaking, sheepishly gathering information he had not been aware of. How stupid he felt, knowing only that his father had died, and nothing of the struggles he had experienced in the leadup.

"Nan died of the same thing," said Leah, "and Dad had been so determined to avoid the same affliction; I'm beyond frustrated for him,"

"He declined so rapidly," Sarah wiped a tear away, "we weren't able to get him into hospice. But please know he was tended to in those final days,"

"Thank you," Leah squeezed her hand.

She's so put together; I don't know how she does it, Locky thought. He moved onto a milk coffee.

"Dementia," said Jacob, "prick of a thing."

The conversation drifted away for a few minutes. Off in the distance the melody of magpies skittered across the countryside atop the low hush of the wind, and the couple's cattle dog, whose name hadn't become known, perked up its ears to sounds unheard to any of them. The clink of tea spoons in cups offered a minor comfort of homely ease; Locky watched as his sister absently rubbed her forearms.

"Well, there's one thing to be said about winter," Jacob finally said, "it's quiet,"

What a useless comment, Locky thought, *small talk, fine, I get it.*

"The cicadas will send you insane in the summertime if you let them,"

Sarah gave him a chastising tap on the thigh, "Shoosh,"

"Yes, well I suppose we'll have to sort out selling the place now," said Leah, "sort through Dad's belongings. All that fun stuff,"

"Unboxing the past," Locky finally spoke, "I wonder if that's tougher than facing the future."

The old couple left in the afternoon; for Leah and Locky, there was an unspoken boost in vivacity given by ordinary conversation amongst the company of others. They looked towards each other wordlessly, perhaps fatuous that they had wasted energy fighting one another, when they were better off building one another up to overcome their shared grief.

"Not sure what we'd have done if they hadn't shown up," Locrian said, "Nobody else here to break up our fight,"

Leah chuckled wryly, "We're the grown-ups now. We have to figure it out ourselves. I think we played nice throughout that visit; wouldn't you say?"

"What do you know, Dad taught us something useful,"

They both laughed briefly at the absurdity of it all; like small children they had fought, as siblings were wont to do.

"It goes without saying. I'm going to miss him," said Leah.

Locrian could only shrug reticently. The few metres distance between the two of them might well have been the expanse of the country. When it seemed nothing would break the silence that pervaded, Leah spoke again,

"I might go set myself up in my room,"

"You're going to sleep in there?"

"Bed's still there, just covered with crap. Dad at least put a plastic sheet over it,"

"Barely any room to turn around though,"

"I think I'll like being surrounded by old junk. It's comforting, I guess,"

She placed a hand on his shoulder before deciding a hug was better, then turned for the stairs.

"Lee,"

"Yeah?"

"Is that why you were late getting here?"

She ran her palm along the stair rail, "Yes. He wasn't too happy about me leaving home. Even for this,"

"I want to help,"

She pondered a moment, wishing she could just announce her misery for sympathy, that she was used to running last, used to carrying everyone else's problems, but instead she simply said, "Let's deal with Dad's stuff first. We'll get to it later."

TWENTY-FIVE

January 2003

The Australian citizen could build a sturdy home to withstand the harsh elements of that southern climate, yet no level of aegis could fully deliver impunity from the fiercest of nature's disasters – the bushfire. Nothing tempered the sword proficiently as the blacksmith's flame, and out the other side of extreme tragedy, the land could purge and renew on a cycle of seasons; each fire leaving with it the wisdom of stories, the knowledge of its potency. A fear of God was the beginning of wisdom, and respect of the flame and its power held in revered stead the man astute enough to adhere.

The bushlands had threatened combustion for months; drought and a hot summer culminated in a fatal day of extreme heat and high winds, and a 'watch and act' alert had been escalated to an emergency warning. The days had been spent dutifully preparing for the homestead a defence against the threat; Charles had stripped the gutters clean of leaves, cleared the surrounding lawns of branches fallen in the wind, and prepped the rainwater tanks with garden hoses that wound the entire perimeter of the house. The hill was steep, and unlike most objects under gravity, a fire would relish the slope, and he knew the pine plantation nearby presented a significant threat of ember attack.

The price of the lifestyle all at once seemed foolish; he felt himself a sitting duck at nature's mercy. Scenic locale, peaceful surroundings, *a threat of death* – a real estate agent wouldn't dare mention the fear of living in one's own home, like a mouse led to a trap. Inside the house, the television had been left on all day, with rolling coverage of the inferno that was spreading out to their west, and the children, now preteens, were heeding their father's warning and packing only their most precious belongings into their suitcases.

Ruth had called her son from her Goulburn home, *leave early*, she had implored, *everything you need is here.* Everything they'd need – who could make such a claim? Locky had surveyed his bedroom; at the guitar that wouldn't fit in the car with *more important possessions*, the stuffed animals that took up a deceptive amount of space in his bag, or the books that he hated to bend or crease to save room.

Better bent than lost for good.

Maggie had said that – his father's new partner. They had been together for about a year now; Locky barely considered the woman, choosing instead to simply accept her presence with a sullen indifference. On the other hand, Leah sculpted herself to the mould of a protégé, one who might teach her of the ways of womanhood – one without the considerable age gap shared between her and her grandmother.

Leave it all behind, your life is more important that anything here.

You're just copying what Maggie said, Leah.

So?

So, it's not as easy as that. I don't want to leave anything behind. It's mine. Who has the right to take it away from me?

Easy enough for Leah to say; the girl held herself at a distance from almost everything, floating from one aspect to another like a cottonweed. For Locky, he saw himself more like a spider, held to one web of being and stubborn to move – or maybe like one of those bower birds who collected trinkets for validation and hoarded them to himself in a hidden nest where nobody could hurt him.

The cicadas filled the reddened sky with their ear-splitting trill, enough to drive a man insane, and the acrid scent of smoke taunted the lurking horror that crept closer to them by the hour, the air around them like a furnace. The car was packed, a life of memories stuffed into a small vehicle – death might rob these items of any value, but they were alive now, and they'd salvage what they could, even if it made for an uncomfortable car ride. The kids crammed themselves into the backseat, satiated by a lunch pack Maggie had made for them both,

It'll be a little adventure.

The sprinklers had been set, spewing a pathetic spray on and around the house, time would tell whether it did anything to protect the home. Charles grunted into the car and shut the door, hands clutching the wheel as he caught his breath.

That's all I can do.

It is. There's every possibility the fire doesn't reach us.

Bit of a pious wish there, Mag.

Better to think that way, I reckon. For the kids.

The ignition turned and Locky watched the house shrink from view as they drove down the hill to the road, trapped behind the glass of the car window, fading, until the trees hid it from view. He tried to prepare for himself the thought of never seeing his home again. Cinders flew erratically betwixt the pines, a fiery fae teasing an awful potential to the trunks that stood sentinel and awaited their terrible fate. They drove beneath power lines that crackled and sparked; Leah pointed to a fruit bat that hung lifelessly from the wires.

It would appear that they weren't the first to think of it. Both roads out of Braidwood — northwest towards Goulburn or east to Batemans Bay — were lined with unmoving cars as far as they could see, segments of some metal centipede. Their progress slowed to a crawl, and above them the sky darkened further with a threatening red, whether it was night or day, such could not be discerned. Locky covered his face with his hands, choked for air in the confines of the car but unable to open the window and bear the horrific smells of the bushfire smoke, of the simmering fuel that burnt from the fumes of the traffic jam. His heart raced; the car was fortunate if it moved a few metres for every minute that passed. Looking out the rear windshield, the horizon glowed the colour of blood, the direction of his home, and when he looked forward to the sluggish progress of his path to salvation, he knew neither road was one he wanted. They were trapped, why could he see it and nobody else? A hand was placed on his knee, his father's, who had looked over his shoulder in the static traffic and seen his son's distress.

I know you're scared, mate. But I'll do everything I can to protect you. That has been my promise to you.

I don't want to go, I want my home, I can't do this.

Sometimes you have to let go of everything. I know it's hard. But we're alive, we're together — we can thank God for another day.

***

It would be on another day, when the winds had dropped and the afternoon sun shone beautifully on the green fields around their home, that their father sat in the loft, eye fixed to the telescope. Within the fishbowl lens a waxing crescent loomed silent, another world that worried not of hellfire or strife. Time had told that the house had been spared of flame, but both house and inhabitants knew that already. Charles recalled being a twelve-year-old boy and knowing there were men up there – men in space. What phase had the moon been in on that day? It seemed like an important point. His daughter played on a Game Boy that spat quirky chip tunes from her bedroom door, barely audible over the jilted piano sounds issued from his son's room.

My children, their little worlds.

His son was practicing scales, each progressively darker than the last, until a certain dissonant tonality caught Charles' attention, and he stood behind his boy and watched in amazement.

They can do things I can't.

His left hand stretching to depress an octave of F-sharp, the boy ran the fingers of his right hand up and down the white keys.

"That's a weird one, mate,"

A startled shudder ran through the boy, he had not heard his father come in.

"It's called Locrian,"

"No kidding," replied Charles, "I'm not sure it works,"

"Everywhere I read, it says the same thing – don't use Locrian mode. Why is it here though? How can it have no purpose? There's seven of these things, and only six of them function,"

"Leftovers, I guess,"

Lowering his left hand by a semitone, he resumed playing the same notes, but with an F-natural instead.

"That's nicer," said Charles.

"It's Lydian," replied Locky.

"Yes. Lydian."

TWENTY-SIX

Thursday, 14 August 2025

During the night, he dreamed. He dreamed that his teeth were falling out of his mouth. From a peculiar fullness inside his mouth, a shifting of foundations, his drooling lips split forth pearls of blood-clotted calcification; sea-sponge gums revealing the jagged root of tooth that had meant to remain unseen. Some of them required a second examination, a prodded fingertip around his palm – reading his future, counting his coins – there were more teeth than a human mouth could contain. Sometimes another glance would reveal them to be marbles, clear as glass, perfectly smooth spheres, with an occasional odd sort that might be of a deep red or black. His head folded forward, teeth falling, unable to be stopped, completely robbing him of any control.

As a child he had read *The Hobbit*, and held an adoration for a particular chapter involving riddles;

Thirty white horses on a red hill,

First they champ,

Then they stamp,

Then they stand still.

Had Bilbo said that, or was it Gollum?

Gollum or Smeagol? she asked, *Flat-five or sharp-four? I don't remember; I should really get around to reading it again.*

How is it that you're here? he asked.

Because you don't fail what you know, she said.

You left me here alone. When I need you most, you were gone.

Gusts struck upon the door to his heart until the ribs cracked and the gale blew in unabated. There his heart teetered on the precipice of salt-sting mourning; the way out was no longer through, rather up the oyster-sharp incline of a knuckled crag, or down and dashed on the jagged precipice below. His icy love had flown in on the rare snow, yet this was only a dream, reality would confirm her absence.

In another life, I was an Eastern Koel.

Those aren't your eyes.

Heard of 'em? They're a type of cuckoo bird; they lay their eggs unbeknownst in the nest of another creature.

That voice is not your own.

A brood parasite! And me and my feathered kin would delight in kicking the eggs out of the nest, cackling as they cracked on the earth below — teeth a fallin', sunny side up.

This house is not a home.

Lighten up. Like you've never broken into an abandoned house. Nobody is home to kick you out, or even notice you're squatting.

You'll ruin everything.

I can't ruin the ruined. The die was cast long before you could ever intervene.

Bereft the day lamented its faded azure, and again he bled alone without a cure. God damn those ugly eyes; God damn that poisoned thought that snuffed the flame from whence it came.

Still, I'm here. And still, I'll stay.

I despise you, fool.

Sea's too rough to skip stones.

If you wouldn't listen to me, would you at least hear yourself?

Go away. You left me here with nothing. You don't get to tell me nothing.

Nothing, nothing – you can count your blessings as they come, but are you counting down your days that go the other way?

Leave, Chimera; hold your starlight at bay.

You knew I'd play my tricks.

I knew I'd fall for them, too.

He laughed to think of it; someone else had pointed it out to him – people were born upside-down. Nobody could run the race until they turned themselves around and rose to their feet. How could anyone hope to save themselves when they weren't even facing the right way? At least the grass was growing, little florid blades in the snow, from out the world the parent leaves behind.

I can't go on under this violent star.

I can see your screams.

Your snow-capped star.

Walk into my seas.

Swirling in the unruly swell, unfurling wet sails and hoping they'd catch on impartial trade winds. The waves were higher when he'd come down to meet them, rising around him in a concave. The horizon kept moving with him, never closer. He could only swim so long before the bloated swell consumed him.

Help me.

Don't let it get you down, Flat-Five. The dream will end soon. It's time to wake up.

How can I walk tomorrow after what I saw today? Why should I trust you?

Trust me? Trust the sun. It will rise whether you like it or not — that violent star of yours.

TWENTY-SEVEN

Thursday, 14 August 2025

Although he could not place it, Locrian felt a pervading sense of dread hanging in vapours about the morning, that a split in the corridor approached and choosing the wrong direction to look first would leave him vulnerable to any beast that might lurk around the corner. Beneath him, his feet proceeded involuntarily up the timber steps with great care made to avoid making a sound. There were enough hints of it anyway – a muttering of voices, a scratching at the walls, the wind seeking concealment in the darkled corners of the house which shuddered in protest of its touch.

Within the walls of his head, Locrian's pulse pounded; the throb of his blood churning out a rhythmic chanting of voices that echoed out in an insomniac's rondo. The fractured sleep he'd gathered throughout the week had pressed him into waking hours plagued with heightening anxiety. Still came the muttering of voices, of moths shaking clotted wings on the borders of his blurred reality, and one voice that he recognised as his sister's came muted from behind the cheap gyprock walls of the second storey. It was her voice, her sample of sounds meeting his strained ears in a half of conversation, for she spoke to somebody that he himself could not discern. She had locked herself into the dusty confines of her old bedroom, and from out behind the shield of those childhood belongings she impressed upon the unknown conversationalist a voice firm and reasonable, seasoned with fear.

"I've told you what I need to do,"

Silence.

"That's the plan. I can't –"

Silence.

"If you would please listen,"

Silence.

"I can't control that. Can't click fingers,"

Silence.

"You know how to do that. You don't need me there to –"

Silence.

"Of course I miss her. Don't be ridiculous,"

Locrian caught himself eavesdropping and shook his head, he knew he shouldn't intrude on private conversations. The sound of Leah's footsteps started suddenly, and he frantically slipped into his own bedroom – if she saw him, he could say he was looking for something. The door opened just as his foot struck against a pile of books that clattered on the floorboards.

"All sorted with the solicitor," said Leah, as though she'd already known her brother was there, "he'll meet us in Queanbeyan this morning,"

"Is that who you were talking to now?"

"Huh? You eavesdropping?"

"Sorry, I heard your voice and thought I'd check,"

"You're a terrible liar, bro,"

She was downstairs before he could say anything, noisily searching the kitchen cupboards as though she'd never moved out. The child-made coffee cup remained on the same shelf where Locky had found it the other day, and she clasped at it with a smile.

"That's adorable," she said, "we're going to find a lot when we go through everything,"

"I couldn't believe he still had it,"

"Look, you didn't even spell your name correctly on it,"

"What do I know?" he laughed nervously, then to change the topic, "Sleep ok?"

Leah shrugged, "Reckon there're rats in the walls. Barely slept out of fear of being eaten alive,"

"Well," he replied, "thank God for another day, am I right?"

She wasn't listening, continuing to rummage through the pantry. She procured a pair of wine bottles coated in dust.

"Thank God," she smirked, "This will be required later today; care to join me?"

Locky stammered.

"Relax, Lock; no alcohol, I know. I'll drink your share. Bloody well need it after the week I've had,"

She looked at her wrist watch, "You know what, let's just grab something to eat on the way."

There were very few cars on the road towards Canberra. The grey sky blanketed the countryside with its watercolour strokes, above the pen-scratched sepias of dishevelled highlands that lay oppressed beneath. Leah drove the Corolla, and Locky had been more than willing to oblige, as there was not much that could calm the anguished irritation that taunted at him from the shadows. The road wound through the fields in wide arcs, seemingly never closer to the destination, with the low-lying cloud cover continuing to crush any hope of serenity. Each turn of the wheels was a step towards uncertainty, alongside the road the rail tracks lashed the hills, with rusted mine carts locked to their path. They could surge forward into the darkness of the tunnels or be static in a paralysis of function doomed to remain or retreat – much as Locky was chained to his car seat with words forever unspoken dancing at the back of his throat. Things looked different from his vantage point in the passenger seat – he'd owned the car so long, yet he rarely sat there. To see the slant of the dashboard from another perspective, the other side of the owl figurine that sat beneath the windshield, he felt closer than ever to a certain abyssal maw that loomed forth; his shadow had continued to follow, and would soon overtake him if he did not confront it.

Leah had noticed his vexation, choosing to attribute it to the grief of mourning, for her own burden had become too heavy, and she was reluctant to shoulder any more turmoil, even if it was her brother's.

"I like the owl," she offered.

Locrian turned his head away from the passenger window.

"Oh. A friend gave it to me,"

"You need a friend who'll buy you a new car; I can't believe you still have the Corolla,"

"It still works, I guess,"

"Took me a sec to remember manual cars still exist. You don't forget how to drive stick,"

"People remember what they want," he said, "they forget the rest."

They found themselves travelling uphill at a glacial pace, stuck behind an enormous semi-trailer that spluttered its way forth.

Leah huffed impatiently, "Stresses me out, those bloody things. I can't see around it to overtake,"

Locky closed his eyes and tried to slow his heartbeat.

"I want to ask a stupid question, sis," he said, "I should know the answer to it, but humour me. Did Dad ever meet Georgia?"

"Only a few times," she replied wistfully, "I don't think she understands what's happened to her grandfather – too young. She would have been three when she saw him last, so I guess there's a chance she doesn't remember him at all,"

"A chance,"

"I had this foolish idea in my head that I'd show up at Dad's place and he'd just fix everything, you know?"

"Oh?"

"I don't know why; I chose to believe it, I suppose," she added, "then I get here yesterday – it was so quiet. Nothing that I had dreamed, yet everything I should have expected,"

"And what should you expect?"

She thought for a moment, "If I knew the answer, I wouldn't have to dream."

Under the dull drapery of the grey day, a town like Queanbeyan issued no mirth, and why should it? A rural city turned outer suburb of Canberra was under no obligation on any idle weekday to impress its visitors with anything more than a passing glance, an acknowledgment of one's existence, so long as that one would stay in line. The sky had threatened to rain all morning, yet had so far spared the tired landscape of its sleet. The CBD was a thoroughfare, inviting few folks to stop, preferring to remain unnoticed with the veiled threat of minding one's own business. The Corolla came to a stop right outside the building, Leah and Locky moving swiftly to remain in the cold air for as little time as necessary, with a thrusting of burning hands into pockets, and scarves pulled tighter about their person.

The office of Mr. Bellchambers was another in a line of bleary rooms, where open door policy and glass walls was meant to give rise to comradery but instead gave off the impression of a zoo. Here was the local businessman in his natural habitat, of wasted paper and ink, of pens that never worked when you needed them to. The laminated cardboard of name tags held to office doors with blu-tack – as though to name the man would give him purpose – could so quickly be removed and replaced by the next employee to wander into that trap, and Bellchambers himself was a man who needed no first name – for nobody really cared one way or another.

"Another Smith," he gestured them to sit before his desk.

The smell of mint failed to conceal the exhalations of the morning's coffee, and both brother and sister silently endured the cud-chewing of the man's gum rolling about in that sickly mouth.

Can you do the talking? Locky's expression conveyed to Leah.

Let me do the talking, was her own thought as neither of them spoke aloud.

"We're not entirely sure of the process with all this," she said, "but our dad has passed away and we needed to see his will,"

Bellchambers' head was turned downwards to his keyboard, eyes looking from under furrowed brow at Leah, "And are you the executor of the estate?"

Leah shrugged, "They were words Dad said to me, not that I know what it all means. Kind of hoped you'd share a bit of your expertise there,"

"Right," the man's chest puffed, "let's see what we have here on file,"

Locky nudged his foot against Leah's, rolling his eyes subtly once he'd caught her attention. A sticky clacking of keys filled the room, bouncing off the glass walls as nameless employees drifted past, each taking their moment to glance emotionlessly at them. Locky could hear Leah's breath whistling softly through her nose; the fluorescent battens above them flickered sporadically, although both Leah and Bellchambers seemed not to notice.

"Revocation," Bellchambers muttered, "trustee, you are the daughter Leah – blah, blah, blah, standard stuff,"

Locrian shifted in his seat, one of the armrests was broken and he had no idea where to place himself. He crossed his legs both ways, placed his hand on his chin, leaned forward, but could not find his equilibrium. The voice of the solicitor dropped to a barely audible murmur; a dull vibration rattled at Locky's chest, underlain and baritone – a photocopier ground out its industrial moan from somewhere nearby. Again the lights dimmed, and he looked to both his sister and the solicitor for recognition, but neither of them paid any attention to the darkness that shrouded the office, the green of the exit signs, the red of the emergency lights. The sounds he heard were muffled, as though he were underwater, held together by that drone of machinery, a tearing of paper, the somewhat archaic tones of landline phones ringing. If only somebody would notice him, see his torment, validate his suffering – he looked next to him to where his sister sat and saw *she had been replaced by another woman*, her face shrouded in death-deep umbra; she turned her head towards him as he choked on a scream that issued forth in a pathetic whimper. He leaned to where the missing armrest should have been and fell off the chair with a thud. In a flash, the lights were back on, the normal sounds of the office on a Thursday morning returned, and Leah was kneeling beside him.

"The fuck's wrong with him?" asked Bellchambers.

"Lock," said Leah, "Lock, what happened?"

The solicitor was plainly irritated at having to pry hospitality from his slackened sense of appeal, clicking his fingers at the receptionist who looked in at them with concern.

"Can we get some water in here or something?" Bellchambers asked.

When he had gathered himself properly, Locrian blushed with humiliation.

"I'm fine, please. Not necessary,"

"I told them these chairs were a death trap," said the solicitor, clearly wishing only to defend himself, "I have it in writing,"

"He said he's fine, thank you," said Leah firmly.

Bellchambers stood and placed his fingertips on the desk.

"Why don't I get you lot a copy of this will; you might prefer to read it in your own time,"

"Locky," said Leah, "what do we do now? Dad has said he doesn't want a funeral."

TWENTY-EIGHT

June 1997

"I did something dramatic last weekend,"

"Go on,"

"The old greenhouse," said Charles, "I tore the damn thing down,"

Dr. Antony typed away at his computer while Charles leaned forward and rubbed his hands together.

"I know Candace loved it," he continued, "I don't know; I couldn't bear to look at it anymore,"

"Did it give you any clarity?"

Charles smirked, "That was only half of it. I chucked all the timber into a pile and lit it up – great big bonfire in the backyard. Honestly it was very cathartic,"

"My goodness," the doctor's eyes widened, "that *is* rather dramatic,"

"It was a controlled burn, obviously. I knew what I was doing. Now that I say it aloud though, maybe it was foolish,"

"No, I see your intent,"

"You see them backburning all the time near my place; preventing bushfires – or I should say lessening the severity. I guess I saw it as a way to safeguard our future, put aside the awful things that have happened,"

"I often liken that to books scattered on the floor, reorganising them and placing them back on the shelf in their rightful place. Your analogy is much more visceral,"

"Big change needs big change? I don't have the eloquence to say what I mean here. I think you get the picture though,"

"I do, I do," the doctor replied, "Forgive me though – what of Locky? I can't imagine he would be too keen to see fire so close to his home,"

"I knew all that. The kids were at their grandmother's. Don't worry, I'd have never done it if he was around. Wasn't much left for them to see after the burn anyway, I don't think either of them even noticed it was gone,"

He paused for a moment.

"It was kind of like, taking back some control over it,"

"In a very emblematic way, yes," said the doctor.

Charles rubbed his forehead, "I've spent over six years hiding my more volatile emotions from them. All the pain, grief, anger – and I've got to carry on doing so if I ever hope to give them the innocence they deserve as kids,"

"You are very stoic, my friend,"

"What else can I do if not be stoic? I'm only a man though, sometimes I need to breakdown,"

"Perhaps in wake of your little destructive episode, you can turn towards productivity. Repurpose the space where the greenhouse stood,"

"Way ahead of you there, mate. I'm keeping the garden. Candace used to grow the most beautiful roses there; I plan to start cultivating my own,"

"I think that's a wonderful idea,"

"I know it is," Charles had become defiantly animated, "I'll grow as many flowers as I can – for her. I'll stick my hands in the soil, turn it over, grow some giant red tomatoes – anything, I don't know,"

"Gardening is a fantastic way to manage your stress. You can involve the kids as well,"

"I will. And I'll tend that garden until the day I die,"

"Excellent," said Dr. Antony, "A simpler solution than selling your home,"

Charles shrugged, "I was thinking about it the last few months. Just uproot and start anew. I can't though; once I thought hard about it, I realised how much the place means to me. You don't know what something means to you until it's gone, or until you consider what life's like if it wasn't there,"

"It sounds as though your despair has given you insight,"

"It has," Charles trailed off, there was a slight hint of a maudlin smile on his face, "She's still there, my girl. In and around the place; in the bones of the damn house, the wind in the trees, I can tell. I'll never leave her. It was the house we wanted, the house we were going to raise our babies in, grow old in. I couldn't ever go. What more can I say? She's still got me. The house is my keeper."

He drove a distant stare into the teal walls of the office. For that moment, he thought the room was the only place that existed. If he opened the door, looked at the window, he'd see nothing – just darkness, or perhaps a light so bright that nothing else could be seen, all things losing their shape to a boundless infinity.

"God," his voice dropped to a whisper, "How can I ever tell them?"

Dr. Antony looked patiently towards him, sorting through his mind for the right answer, but he could find nothing of value to offer.

He held his composure, "For now, they know enough,"

Charles gazed back at him with tears welling in his eyes.

"There will come a time," the doctor continued, "when they're old enough to be told more. They might approach you. You might gently explain it to them. More importantly, you'll tell them how much she loved them – her children,"

"Plato's cave," said Charles.

"Sorry, what?"

"Plato's cave. I don't know what they see. I want them to understand and not be afraid. But I also want to keep them from danger, shield them. I don't know what to do with that yet. I want them to know how much I love them. That I'm there for them, whatever shadows they see,"

"Are you teaching me philosophy now?" the doctor smiled.

Charles shrugged once more and shook his head absently, "You've taught me a thing or two, mate,"

"Then do that. Love them. Be there for them. Trust them to understand, your love will come across to them in ways unsaid."

The room exhaled the silence, taking with it another small portion of his suffering away into the aether, and the burden Charles carried became marginally lighter.

Dr. Antony looked at the clock, "Well, we've got about six or seven minutes left – was there anything else you wanted to talk about?"

"I think I'm good for today,"

"Great, until next time then."

TWENTY-NINE

August 2005

The birds flew frozen in a sky of crimson ice, wings flung, crest curled; a time-locked flight without destination, a path repeated in a mirrored pattern up and down the walls of Leah's bedroom. Within her sanctuary things knew their place and confided themselves to the occupant alone; treasures gathered and piled in an orderly chaos, the bed unmade (because she would just sleep there again tonight), clothes in crumpled heaps on the floor (icebergs in a millpond sea), the stack of burned CDs next to the player (track lists written in black sharpie). Everything was where she chose it to be, and nothing would dare misplace itself without her volition. The room had to remain this way, this refuge from the life that circled like sharks – *out there* – in the wide world she felt so thrust into. Here she could return and reset, answer to nobody but herself, and only the questions she deemed vital to her felicity. When the hot-tempered girl stormed in suddenly, throwing the door closed with a clumsy slam, those walls could begin their task of imparting their serene calmness – their ataraxia – and silently encircle her with a becalmed embrace.

It had been an increasingly difficult experience for Leah, navigating a channel where she could no longer observe the port of childhood nor see her destination on the horizon. There was an anxiety she could not put into words that had made its chains known to her for as long as she could remember; yet those chains had loosened with the presence of her father's partner Maggie, who had entered their lives three years earlier with a palette of status quo Leah had yearned for.

We're finally a normal family.

Normal – nothing she recognised or seemed capable of, not her. Not those crazy old Smiths in the haunted house, that weird family with the tragic past. Not even the commonality of her last name had been enough for her to blend in. But now her dad had gone ahead and ruined it all; he'd told her that day that he and Maggie had made the decision to part ways.

This is not a choice we've taken lightly.

We understand this might upset you.

No, there's nothing you can do to change it.

It was a magician's trick, a rug pulled out from beneath her, but instead of remaining still to the sounds of awed applause, she had stumbled, sucker-punched by its suddenness and unable to process the emotions that pressed forcefully on her. That

Maggie had not even been there to tell her, gone already like it was nothing – therein lay the true pain, the coup de grace from which she'd need to once more recover, once more squash down the hurt if she intended to carry on.

I'm sure we'll still speak from time to time; it's not as though she ever lived here with us. Life will be as normal as it ever was.

There was that word again – normal. She could appreciate her father's attempts to understand her, but cursed the failings that he didn't see.

With her face buried in her pillow, hair tossed madly in a heat of frustration that searched for an outlet, Leah screamed and launched her fist into the bed with a thump. Another fist made its own thump, that of a gentle knocking on her door that she resolutely ignored.

"Leah," said her father, "can I come in, love?"

Not unless you fix the mess you made! How often did he tell her to do the same thing when her room was untidy?

The door opened gingerly, and Charles stood in a spot where he could make a swift egress should he receive the order. His hands sheepishly pocketed, his nerves were openly apparent.

"Leah, I know you're upset,"

"Smart one, you are," she sneered.

"I'll cop that," he replied, "Look, I don't know what else to tell you. Sometimes things don't work out for two people. The good times get a bit unbalanced with things you can't see eye to eye on,"

She sat up on her bed and cleared her eyes, "Well then, make it work out. You tell me and Lock all the time to stop fighting,"

Charles dared to laugh lightly, "You guys are brother and sister – family. Family doesn't go anywhere. It's always with you, so better to keep the peace,"

No, that's terrible advice, he thought.

"What I should say is; things can change with the people we choose to invite into our little circle. Mag and I checked in with each other – which is a good thing to do with your partner – and we realised we weren't able to meet each other's needs anymore,"

It made no sense to Leah; adults overcomplicated everything.

"I need her though," she began to cry, "did you think of that when you guys broke up?"

Charles felt a strong urge to make light of her dramaticism – *everything was the end of the world with teenagers* – he caught himself before he made such a fatal error. He surveyed his daughter's room; the Green Day poster on the wall that covered the stain of two-minute noodles spilt accidently, the gossip magazines that lay open on her desk next to her homework – *did her grandmother give her these? God, I really don't understand her at all these days.*

"May I sit?" he placed his hand on the desk chair.

"You're going to anyway,"

He sighed – he could only continue to try and understand.

"You don't have to like me right now," he said, "and you might not believe me when I tell you – I know what it's like to have someone ripped away from you,"

Leah felt a pang of guilt.

"There'll be people in your life who arrive for a given spot of time, only to move on," he said, "That's life. Sometimes they disappear suddenly, other times it's a gradual drift. The true friendships stay with you though. And if it happens that one of those true friendships ends for reasons beyond your control, well, you can keep them with you in here,"

He tapped his chest.

"You have to decide which people you keep around; and you'll know, it's easy to see when you look. Now Mag and I were able to split amicably, that's kind of the best way you could hope – no screaming and shouting,"

Leah felt the anger leave her body; she wouldn't say it then, that she loved him, that she knew she'd keep *him* around,

"So dumb," she said instead, "Guess being stuck with you and Lock isn't so bad,"

"Stuck fast, girl," said Charles, "Our Leah, we're not going anywhere,"

"My dad."

They embraced; there was more Leah wanted to say, but she lacked the words. What she'd said already seemed enough, and she would never know in that moment, that her father couldn't agree more.

In the calm after the storm, she finally spoke again, "Well look at you – back out there having break-ups and heartache,"

"There's a reason why it's a young person's game, let me tell you," he replied.

"Your first girl since Mum,"

He shook his head, "Nope, second,"

Leah looked perplexed.

"You wouldn't remember the first," he said, "only saw her for a few months – you'd have been too young to remember,"

"I had no idea,"

"Your brother might remember, I don't know. He never shares much; it was a year or two after your Mum. I was in no state to be with anyone, so it didn't last long at all,"

"No kidding,"

"Yeah. Lydia. Nice enough woman."

THIRTY

October 2024

The months were consumed, never mind how fast or slow, by a searching of souls, of boxes tipped over in hopes of finding redemption. Locrian and Lydia, thrill-stripped by the banal, exhausted of hope, ambled through the days alone with each other. There no longer appeared to be the possibility of avowal; the reality of an impending rupture increased as their walls disintegrated slowly, the rust gaining advantage in the unseen minutes. There was one explanation, although he didn't dare say it aloud – that she was falling out of love – whatever that meant. To 'fall' in and out of love – he hated the expression. Surely love was chosen and left with confident steps. He bled at the very notion of losing her, and fawned anew with the vigour of a child trying to get the attention of a parent. If she would just tell him what was wrong, he could fix it.

"You already know what's wrong," she said.

"I'm not a mind reader,"

"Ain't that the truth,"

"I want to help,"

"Leave me alone to find the truth myself."

Truth. He tried to remember earlier times, when life had been happy and easy, but he could not. Yet surely there had to have been a moment, a pocket of days unsullied; for how on earth had they endured to this point if not without the promise of returning to what they once found so simple?

"Of course you can't remember. You never hold onto anything when life's peachy," she told him, "Why anchor yourself to a single spot when it's all good?"

Right then he'd have anchored himself to anything. The months were consumed, never mind how fast or slow.

He continued to stare out into the darkness. The darkness stared back at him. It taunted him, danced on the notion that it might conceal something or reveal nothing. Certainly Locrian could reach out into the black, perhaps a salvation stood directly beside him and he could not see; but *should* he reach out? That was another question entirely.

The months were consumed, never mind how fast or slow, by that abyss of oblivion; engulfed greedily by a hungry and eldritch beast, holding memories to itself with a celestial gravity, days hanging like tiny moons trapped in the planetary pull of the wandering star that peered from infinite blackness. Time watched – dilated and wasted – at the change that crept through Lydia's veins, until her eyes were barely recognisable as her own, and Locrian felt her slip slowly away from him.

"I can't see through the veil," he said, "it shouldn't be like this,"

"How long am I to keep up this charade?" she said, "I can't be all that you want me to be,"

He took her hands into his own; the eyes, the eyes that were no longer hers, shifted to avoid his gaze.

"Can I meet you in the middle? My modal palindrome?" he beseeched.

"You vampire of my love," she scolded, "I am none of these things."

Locrian could do nothing but watch as the depression devoured her, his icy love withdrawing further from the joy they'd once shared. Lydia stopped going to work, then stopped getting out of bed at all. Whatever turmoil dwelt within her remained hidden from him, a closely guarded secret he could not guess or vindicate. The months were consumed, never mind how fast or slow.

It became evidently apparent that the darkness that enclosed Lydia was something very different to a fracturing romance. They had reached that point where their wavelengths ran dissonant, out of sync, out of time. For Locrian, the gravity of his own despair dragged him back towards his music, as he clutched at Lydia's old guitar and played a piece that he had recently composed. The strings were dull though, the tuning all wrong, and he was unable to get the tempo right.

"Wrong timing again, Flat-Five,"

How could time be wrong? Reality flickered in and out, a weakening flame.

"Time just passes anyway," he muttered.

Lydia stood over him, the guitar ringing out a single, tuneless chord ad nauseum.

"Time what? What? What? Will you speak up? I can't hear a fucking thing you say, all you do is mumble,"

"Dad once told me something he read," he said, "that time was a frozen river. A big block of ice. Slice it up in anyway, and you can have past, present and future all together at the same time,"

"Gibberish," she said, "from an old man,"

"When he looked through his telescope and pointed at some faraway planet – that light was old, I was looking into the past. If I thought hard enough, I could consider myself in a world where everything that ever was and ever will be was, was – was right now,"

"You're stuttering,"

"I'm echoing,"

She threw her arms in the air, "If I could take back every word I said – let me out of your echo chamber."

He began to consider the real possibility of breaking up with Lydia, what it might look like, whether she'd truly be gone or not. The months were consumed, never mind how fast or slow.

When he first noticed her self-harming, it took him by surprise. It was a shadow on her wrist, a swelling of broken cells, a burn that had torn a small strip of her away where it would rise like smoke into nothingness.

"Before you say what you're thinking," she said, "it isn't something you should concern yourself with,"

"What the fuck, Lyd," he took her hand gently, "what is this?"

"I was cooking; boiling water splashed at me,"

"Tell me the truth,"

"I burnt my wrist with the lighter. It helps me feel, feel, feel alive,"

Her voice stuttered echoes in the vacuum of his skull.

"You don't need to do this," he implored of her, "Please, don't. Let me help, you know all of my light is for you,"

She looked at him through a veil of tears, "Why won't you let go? I'm already gone,"

"I will stand with you. Watch you until dawn; your vigil,"

"What hope are you, when you can't even see in the dark."

It was not a question, but a statement.

"Nothing is coming," he said, "nothing is coming to –"

"Save. You."

"Nothing is lurking in the dark. I can protect you."

The blinds in their flat had remained down for longer than either could remember; day was night, and the months were consumed, never mind how fast or slow.

From out the foetid darkness of dream-drowned sleep the storm tossed up visions of cruel hatred. Her eyes, those eyes that weren't her own – and their flat, no longer home. Her voice came to him, unfamiliar in its tonality; still her, still there, but all wrong.

"Do you fear your home betraying you?"

He had been trying to sleep; through his blurred eyes the clock glowed of the witching hour. Lydia stood at the window; the streetlight gave her an outline, but no more detail than shadow.

"I think about the solitary hour of a person's death. Walk to the light, they say. Why would one see a light? They couldn't. Close your eyes and there is no light,"

Locrian spoke uninhibited by waking reality, his brain sponged in a miasma of sleep, "You could build a fire,"

"I don't want to see,"

"I can fix it,"

"I don't need you to tell me how to land when I fall."

That following day, whatever day it might have been, a man named Locrian Smythe readied himself for work. The months had been consumed, never mind how fast or slow, and he was determined to haul himself out of the rut and take back the life that was bleeding out from him. Tapping a vein of enthusiasm, he approached the day with the desire to share of his found joy – that rare treasure – with the woman he loved and yearned to encourage.

"Let's do one thing today," he said, "one thing; it doesn't have to be big. Just a single step. Any direction will do,"

But for Lydia, time had dilated to the point where a minute was eternity.

"Do you ever worry about what you might do in a moment of madness?"

A man named Locrian Smythe went to work that day. He went to work to forget. He ignored the voice that called him back home.

"To light a fire. She's death dressed up as life."

There was nothing going on to suggest it was a day of any significance, not externally at least, in the office where muted greys were the order of business, and the hours were consumed, never mind how fast or slow. The man named Locrian Smythe drank his coffee, attempted small talk with his colleagues, ignored the comments made about his appearance. He had to get something done, anything to give value to himself and the day, lest it melt like a berg in the sea, consumed by the amorphous mass of ocean. He'd win the bread, take home the bacon, present himself to his love – hold his art under his chin for her to see.

Built around him in panels was his workspace, one of many mirrored down the corridors of the open-plan office, where the furthest from him housed the silhouette of his icy love, still clouded of detail from last night's shadow; the eyes that weren't her own stared at him from that darkness. But she shouldn't be here. Not here. He stood and rushed over to her, paying heed to his discretion, praying he would remain unseen by his colleagues yet understanding the urgency of reaching her before she ruined everything.

"You let me in," she said.

She smiled; her face unveiled. There she was – his dusky jewel – of all things, smiling. There was no malice, no sadness, just his Lydia, the harmony to his dissonance; his heart might bleed to capture it, but not here. She couldn't be here.

"Why are you here?" he hissed.

"You locked me in,"

"You –"

She spoke over him, "You threw away the key. Into an enharmonic river,"

He shook his head fiercely, "Stop. Please, don't.

"You can't change it."

Locrian groaned inwardly, the heads around him turning, the mumbling commotion of his faceless colleagues gathering concern for wellbeing both theirs and his own.

"No, you're not really here,"

"And you're not really Locrian. Are you?"

"Stop. Please, don't."

"I'm just a face from your past, aren't I?"

He screamed, and felt his arms grabbed by a pair of faceless employees – his friends? – he didn't know.

"Look Lachlan,"

Was he sitting? How did he get here?

"We're just a little bit concerned about your wellbeing,"

"No,"

"And think it's best for everyone if we stand you down,"

"Where is she?"

"Get yourself right. Take some time,"

"Is business slow?"

"Sure, mate. Business is slow."

It was evening when he left. A man named Lachlan Smith wandered home, wandered aimlessly, drawn along the string of streetlamps where moths flitted in and out, perilously close to the heat of the globes. He knew the way home, whether he realised it or not; he did not need to hurry, he was already early, already late. Perfunctorily ambling, one step after another to the second storey above the jazz bar – closed on this night – to procure the key in his hand and unlock the door to his home, a key he never considered until he needed it. A strange smell filled his nostrils; ominous, sinister, and again the silhouette appeared, this time in the hallway. The silhouette lit by the slanted blinds seeping the barest of light from the streetlamps. The silhouette of an old man that stood in the hallway. His father, but no – how could that be? The pallid face, the sallow cheeks, the sunken eyes – a cheap imitation of his father – death dressed up as life. Wordlessly they stared at one another; his father, standing in the hallway, standing in his way. Lachlan stepped towards him, down the hallway, his footsteps echoing on the floorboards, eyes never leaving the old man, until he made to pass the frozen figure. In a movement that startled him, Lachlan felt his father's hand on his arm. Was he being disciplined? Was he being guided? Warned? Protected? The mouth of the old man, sickly and slow, looked as though it wanted to form speech but struggled to spit the words from his throat. One word, a single croak, slid out of his lips,

"Wait."

The son watched his father twitch and attempt to take a step. But he was too old, and he couldn't move himself from the hallway, couldn't carry on beyond the liminal space between the rooms. He could only look despairingly at his son and watch as he left him behind and entered the bedroom.

She was there. There was a look over her shoulder, the rest of her body followed. What was it that she held in her hand? His heart lurched; the bed lay between them, and he knew in an instant that he couldn't get to her in time.

"Please, don't." his voice desperate in his defeat.

"I'm sorry, baby boy."

The lighter was dropped, ignited by life, and his icy love went up in flames before his eyes.

THIRTY-ONE

Thursday, 14 August 2025

A half dozen sheep had broken through the wire fence to graze absently and observe the Corolla that rounded the driveway. The seventh, a ram, gave one scuff of its hoof as if to imply that they would not be moving along any time soon. The brother and sister, alone with one another, were too exhausted to shoo them away. The drive home had felt an eternity of wordless tension, as there was not much either could have said, and the news of their father's refusal of a funeral seemed to set them back rather move them forward. Although he may not have noticed it, Locky's younger sister gave him an occasional sidelong glance, one of concern, after he had experienced a rather unusual episode at the solicitor's office. Leah's eyes studied her brother's manner as she drove, as much as she could at least, and Locky in turn did his best to diminish the severity of his fractured psyche.

The sun had set, its light as good as dead as they stretched weary legs and returned aching bodies through the mouth of house on the hill. Locky searched his duffel bag, looking for nothing in particular, just a killing of time, while Leah set herself cross-legged before the fireplace to reignite the flame. The sound of kindling cracked and twigs snapped cut the air with a sharp staccato of sound.

"Are you going to tell me what happened?" she finally asked.

What happened – Locky managed to confuse himself, stumbling upon a recollection of a thousand memories, trying to uncover which one his sister was talking about.

"I get that this is a pretty stressful time," she said, taking a route of compassion, "but you need to pull yourself together, I can't do all this myself,"

He knew she was right, and wished he could do as such; to pull himself together – he'd tied himself in knots trying to do it alone.

"I've been seeing things," he managed to say, "grief will do that, I suppose,"

Leah stood and dusted her hands; the fire was lit and slowly uptook its task of warming the hollowed room.

"Ghosts aren't real. Reality is frightening enough."

The sheep had gone by nightfall, replaced by the haunted echoes of owls that periodically made themselves known. Leah sat on the veranda outside the main living space and worked her way through the first of several wine bottles she had discovered earlier. Locky could see her there, in the comforting concealment of shadows, his final friend, another who he might push away in time without his personal intervention. Despite this, he just sat there on the lounge near the fire, the television turned on only to fill the air with a noise that might drown out his thoughts.

"I was thinking," he now stood in the open glass doorway.

Leah was jolted from her reverie.

"Sorry," he said, "didn't mean to startle you,"

She looked at him and said nothing.

"What if came to live over there, in South Australia, I mean?"

"What about your job?"

The job I was stood down from? Medically unfit — they said.

"Could get a transfer," he said.

Leah seemed to consider it; that her brother might step in and white knight all her problems, but no, such was a fairy-tale, and she was no damsel – it was a laughable notion.

"How's the footy?" she pointed to the television, "Grand final rematch or something? See, I know sport,"

He could hear the slur in her voice; one of the wine bottles was almost empty. She gestured him to sit.

"You should join me; I know you don't drink, but if you don't want to get drunk after today, maybe you're stronger than you think you are,"

Locky fixed his gaze on the bottle – no, even tonight he couldn't handle that burning sensation he despised so much.

Leah shook the bottle, teasing him, "Don't fear the reaper," before slamming it down harder than she intended.

"You know," she slurred, "he's expecting me back home tomorrow. Might as well have dropped me at Canberra Airport while we were in there today. Even now, he won't let go,"

"I should have paid closer attention," said Locky, "I'm sorry,"

"Don't be – I'm having a blast. Isn't that ridiculous? My dad's dead, my husband's a monster and I'm sitting here getting wasted – time of my life,"

"If you're not laughing, you're crying,"

"Bro, what's the bloody point of family? All we do is hurt one another. We can barely stand ourselves long enough to be alone, then too pre-occupied with our own problems to ever work together,"

"You think I'm in any position to give wisdom here?"

"You never know, you might be a philosophical drunk. Here's one – how's that old Australian proverb go? Ah yes – *Shit's fucked*,"

Locky wasn't sure he liked drunk Leah, but she wasn't through yet.

"I wonder all the time if I've done my daughter a tremendous disservice by bringing her into this world," she turned to look at him, "Do you think she'd hate me if she knew? God – *when* she knows?"

Knowing he could add nothing encouraging, Locky shifted in his seat and sought to change the subject.

"How can he expect you back so soon? We've still got to tell the mortuary what's going on. Wouldn't it make better sense to stay here until we have things sorted?"

"You don't have to tell me, Lock," she shook her head, "I'm pissed off at Dad. Why would he refuse a funeral? It's selfish. A funeral is for us, for us to grieve – it makes no sense to put that in your will,"

The music of the night played softly beyond the lighted windows of the house. The moon was just past full, rising in the eastern sky without any expectation of attention.

Leah broke the silence, "When I told my boss that Dad had died, that I needed some time off, she asked me how old he was. *Sixty-seven,* I say. *So young,* is her response. I almost laughed. Dad got twice as many years as Mum, yet both of them 'died young,'"

"I think we all die young," replied Locky, "When you think about it. Or at least we all get long enough – the same sample of miniscule years,"

The temperature had dropped, but neither of them cared. Leah warmed her blood with the alcohol that swirled in her veins, and for Locky, the cold felt appropriate to his mood.

"I was thinking," said Leah, "if Dad's going to be a stubborn bugger and refuse a funeral, maybe we should leave him here with Mum, you know – scatter his ashes on the grave,"

"Grave?"

"At the back of the property,"

"Mum's grave," said Locky.

"Yes,"

"At the back of the property."

He stared at Leah; brow furrowed; he had chosen to forget the owner of the gravestone. The emotions that stirred inside him, too painful to unearth, had instead buried themselves deeper into the amygdalic void. To hear them spoken so plainly – *their mother's grave at the back of the property* – shifted the foundations he had balanced himself on for longer than he could remember. The smell of the flame burning in the fireplace brought tears to his eyes that he hid from Leah, faced turned away from the house so that he was half-shadow, half-light. His sister, senses dulled by drink, didn't quite register the visible change that overcame Locky in silent, convulsing sobs.

"He's full of secrets, that Dad of ours," she said, "Wasn't until I turned eighteen that he even told me what happened to Mum,"

Locky choked on the words that had at last risen from deep inside him; they sat in the back of his throat as he forced them forward, "He never needed to tell me,"

Even in her inebriated state, Leah could no longer overlook the deluge of tears that tore down Locky's face, as all function left his body, and the walls of the delusion lasting three and a half decades caved in around him.

"I already knew what happened. She self-immolated. I saw her do it. I was three years old and I saw her do it. And I never told anybody. And I never said it out loud until right now."

THIRTY-TWO

April 1991

The die had been cast – crucially – upon the back of several decisions made that day; decisions that could never have been discriminated as being of any importance at all. The actions of one man, who had recently become a father for the second time, were nothing beyond the norm. The fact that they had run out of nappies for the baby wasn't unusual, nor was the bank account sagging into negative balance under the sheer weight of horribly ordinary bills. A poor night sleep had become the expectation, as he and his wife had wrestled with the fledgling emotions of a newborn and her toddler brother; the children's grandmother could hardly have been blamed for being unavailable to babysit on that day, that particular day that wasn't meant to be unlike any other.

So it was that the man drove his car along the quiet highway, with the mid-morning sun shining like it always had, and the acrid smell of bushfire denoting the backburning that was going that day. The conditions had been right for the controlled burns that promised protection to the inhabitants of the highland countryside. The scent of the blaze, the haze of smoke that clung to the air, these were unpleasant sensations, but nothing more. To the best of his knowledge, the worst of it had been calmed. His wife, his beloved wife, left for that brief reprieve of duty, left to be given sleep that was so sorely needed and deserved, because the children would be fine. Everything was fine. The baby girl slept in her bassinet in the main room. Their son, their little explorer, pre-occupied with the toys he had been penned in with, and the television that played at a low volume nearby.

It's ok, love. A small amount of TV won't rot his brain. Of course he's content, look at him quietly playing. I won't be long at all. Yes, he's had his breakfast. When I get back from the shops, we'll have some lunch.

But our baby.

Look at her sleep. Should have seen the nappy after that last feed — weighed as much as she does. Please, get some rest. You need it.

Of course, they'd been aware of the challenges they'd face in having a second child. Naturally, they'd spoken of the particular issue they'd faced with the birth of their son — the emergence of a post-partum depression that the new mother had fought so hard to manage.

What if it happens again?

We have a wonderful little boy — maybe he's enough.

He deserves a sibling; he shouldn't grow up alone.

He'll never be alone. You've done so well. You can overcome anything.

They knew there would be things they'd just have to make work. They could remember the financial strain of a single income, the time spread thinly between keeping the roof over the heads of the children, the maddening deprivation of basic needs and functions – the sleep deficits, the hours gone with aching arms soothing troubled babies, the four walls of the house turned tortuous as meals were taken quickly and late; the showers taken in minutes bought; the same bed clothes worn and stained with sour milk.

Let me fix it.

You have to work tomorrow.

So do you.

He knew the sacrifices she made for them and wished desperately to give her a world where she was not only recognised, but given the breaks she so sorely needed.

Look, mate. I get it, wife and kids at home. But we need you at work on time.

I'm sorry. Bub was sick right when I was leaving, and the young fella spread his brekky all over the table. The missus appreciates the help.

I'll bet she appreciates the pay cheque we give you too.

They could be a touch more realistic; he'd thought to himself. The children would be this small for only a brief period, blink and it's done; the greater pain would be to miss it. The man had decided to take the day – a gut instinct more than anything else – *no mate, can't make it in today, both kids upset all night, nobody has slept. I will make up the time when I can, I hope you understand.*

Only once it became noticeable that his wife's demons had returned, did the man begin to feel himself stretched to a point of critical failure. The days sat on a knife-edge where one slip could send them spiralling, and they walked the fine line of building one another up as lovers do, even if it meant sacrificing those little parts of self that made them whole.

I scalded my wrist on the baby's bottle.

Are you sure about that?

Look, it doesn't matter, I'm fine now.

At first, she had tried to conceal just how poorly she was doing, because really,

What do you have to complain about?

Oh, you'll miss this one day.

You should be so grateful.

If only they'd admit their own struggle, that raising young children was never the happy dream it was presented as, that everyone hid their inner torments for sake of appearing 'all-put-together'.

I lost the baby weight in under six months.

I was back at work and juggling motherhood as soon as I left the hospital.

Oh, you're so lucky. My husband doesn't help me at all.

People were better off minding their own business; he had told her. She had put on the mask; told him it didn't affect her. The guttural crying behind the bathroom door told him otherwise.

Please, give me the lighter. I'm taking it off you, ok. You don't need to do this.

I'm just all sixes-and-sevens. They'd be better off without me.

Never. How could you say that; you are loved, you are our world.

And they are my bright stars in a dark night.

Other times, the conversation would not resolve in a positive manner.

She's a baby. He's little. They'll forget me. They'll be happier without me.

His heart bled for her, and he could have screamed his devotion to her. He cried for her, begged her to come back, *we'll make it work, we'll get through it together*, but he could only plead from tear-stained eyes; *please, don't.*

Sometimes it feels like I'm already gone.

Through the heightened vigilance of anxiety pulling his heart like a lead weight, he felt a momentary panic when he returned home and found his son was missing. The smell of the bushfires was more intense than ever, and his son was missing. But no, he must be upstairs with his mum; he'd clambered himself onto the safety gate before, but there was no way he could climb over it completely, surely not. No, there was no need to panic. Candace would have woken up from her sleep and was probably playing with him in another room. The baby girl continued to sleep in the bassinet, although the occasional twitch of her little face told that she'd wake soon. It was all a matter of logic, of the most likely solution being the correct one. Charles cursed himself – of all things to forget, he'd forgotten the nappies. He stood, frustrated at his forgetfulness; foolish and sleep-deprived – his family deserved the best he could be; he needed to stay alert, focus on what each of them needed. He could do it; he would do it; he'd slipped up today, forgotten an essential at the shops, it was not a big deal, he could go back.

Once he started to unpack the grocery bags, he became aware of a strange sound – the baby waking? – No, this was coming from the kitchen. From the glass doors of the veranda outside he noticed a trail of dirt leading to the cupboard beneath the sink, where the strange sound was coming from. The trail of dirt, the trail of a child's footprints, leading to the cupboard beneath the sink, where the strange sound came from his son who hid there. He felt his breathing quicken, his heart beginning to race, as he wordlessly removed his boy from under the sink and held his shaking form in his arms. But he was so little, there was no way he could have climbed out of the playpen, no way he was strong enough to do such a thing yet. He couldn't have wandered outside by himself, dirtied up his beautiful little feet. It was not a thing to worry about, the logical explanation would be the correct one – although it was now a delusion that threatened to cave in on itself.

He took Lachlan to the playpen and placed him gently near the bassinet, the boy's eyes staring vacantly through him, *beyond* him, staring through the window to the backyard. Charles toyed with the sinister idea that his wife might no longer be upstairs, that perhaps she was out there, where their son was staring, outside of the house they'd bought for their family. A blood-curdling dread turned in his stomach. In the warm day, he felt unbelievably cold.

He looked at his boy.

"Wait."

She must be in greenhouse. She must have stepped out to tend to the flowers. It was a logical explanation. The doctors had suggested she take up gardening, take those little moments for herself when she could; it was a simple panacea to a problem that didn't need to grow too large. The smoke of the fires came with strength at the turn of the wind – unpleasant, but nothing intolerable. It was smoke from the backburning, there was no way the smoke came from anywhere closer. He would find her in the greenhouse. That's where she would be. She would be tending to the flowers. It was a reasonable explanation. He would find her in the greenhouse. This wasn't really happening, he thought.

Inside the house, he could hear the baby sending cries to her mother that would go unanswered.

THIRTY-THREE

June 2006

To have a birthday on a week night was awkward. It was a five of seven chance any given year, yet nobody seemed to mention how terribly common and anticlimactic this was. For a milestone birthday, like his son's eighteenth, to fall on a Wednesday, a school night, seemed wretchedly unfair. The other kids (and truly they were still kids) would be unlikely to go out and celebrate with Lachlan – too much study to be done in this year, the year of their higher school certificate, and too few with their driver's license to be travelling into town. In a way, Charles had felt sorry for the boy, that was until he'd approached Lachlan about any desired celebrations and received such a milquetoast response.

"Nah, RSL is pretty boring on a week night,"

"And what would you know about that?"

"Nan took us there a few times. Just trivia and soggy fish and chips,"

"You've got me there, son. We can just celebrate at home then,"

"I'll go out," Leah had added, "you can pick me up later,"

"Nice try, girl," Charles replied, "you'll get your chance soon enough,"

His daughter had sulked at what she deemed a missed opportunity, and instead resorted to a reluctant hug and a mumbling of *happy birthday* to her big brother.

So it was that Lachlan simply went to school, because it was the thing to do, and quietly accepted the well wishes, prayed for the day to end, prayed for the spotlight of attention to shift away from him. His father wasn't going to let him off that easily though; this was his boy turned young man, and he wanted nothing more than to make it known just how pleased his was to have him for a son, how much he filled the old man's heart with joy. But it was never quite so forward with teenagers – to show them any level of emotion, they'd merely retreat, mutter their embarrassments and bemoan how their father would *never understand them.*

He had to make it special – this was a rite of passage, he'd only become an adult once in his life, why could Lachlan not see the importance of marking such an event? Yet he agreed to a first beer with the dad, an ulterior motive for Charles to impress upon him the perils of alcohol misuse. It was a fine evening for it; the air still pleasant in wake of the approaching night's cool, the sun hanging low in the western winter sky, the stillness of the trees reflecting those fading rays of gold to the distant melody of kookaburra calls as the two of them sat on the veranda.

"Cheers, son,"

Locky had watched his dad partake of the ritual many times, often with Nan, and to now hold the smooth glass bottle in his hand was an unusual sensation. There did seem to be some sort of appeal to the satisfying sound of glass clinking, the fizz of the elixir within, and the lucid greens and browns of the glass itself.

"It's fucking gross,"

"Lock! Mate, just because you're an adult now, doesn't mean you speak like that,"

"Sorry,"

"Ah, whatever. Just don't do it in front of me or Nan, ok?"

He let out a surprised laugh, "Ha, no worries, Dad,"

"Oh, and Leah," Charles added, "that girl doesn't need any more encouragement with profanities,"

"Too late, Dad,"

"No matter, Lock. Nobody actually likes drinking these things – especially the first one,"

In all honesty, Locky had never really thought about why adults drank alcohol, beyond it being simply *what they did.*

"Just," he said, "it burns. I don't like how that feels,"

He grimaced and rubbed at his throat.

"That's barely the first of it too," replied Charles, "too much and you'll start saying and doing some pretty silly things. Not me, of course,"

"Saint,"

His father smirked, before a change fell over his demeanour.

"You know, it goes without saying – we're very proud of the man you've become, Lock,"

Lachlan, leaning forward, rocked his head about in discomfort.

"I mean it, mate. Just let me say it, ok? Your mum and I love you dearly; there's no doubt you'll do great things,"

No doubt? He wondered how his dad could be so certain, watching the old man shuffle awkwardly in his seat, looking about with a sudden nervousness he didn't understand.

Charles sorted through the thoughts in his head; this was a moment he'd lived out internally so many times across the years, and now the day of his son's eighteenth had finally arrived, he was no longer able to build himself up to speak. His voice shook with nerves and drink.

"You know, son; the day you were born was the happiest day of our lives, your mum and I – Leah's birth, too, I should say. And uh, well I don't know, maybe you have questions about Mum that I could answer for you,"

Locky stared out into the trees that had presently lost their lustre of sunlight to the dusk, "No, not really,"

The response took Charles aback somewhat, the many rehearsed conversations he'd had in his mind over the years had all slipped away at that moment.

"You ever want to talk about her not being around? Not physically, I mean," Charles stumbled over his words.

"I don't really know what I'd do with that information," replied Locky.

A thought emerged for Charles, an old one, an uncomfortable intrusion – that questioned how much his young son had seen on that day, how much he even remembered, having only been a toddler. *I don't really know what I'd do with that information* – did that imply that he'd seen nothing at all? It was a hopeful notion, if not forlorn, and Charles prayed that it might be true, that what he should say to his son would become clear. He'd made it transparent over the years that he was an open door for his children – he might now tell an adult Lachlan there and then of the details of that horrible day, but what would that accomplish, whether the boy was aware or not of the specifics? If not distress, what would speaking it aloud accomplish? There was little more he could do, having probed about, and having his son decline the offer to have any new revelation unveiled.

Charles felt frustrated; the conversation hadn't gone as he'd intended, nothing in life ever did. He had more to write, but his page was already full of words, and the fading daylight made it impossible to see. In that moment he felt no closer to reconciling his family's sufferance. Perhaps it was a journey he'd never complete, so he'd be better off taking in the sights along the way, concerning himself only with the love he held for his wife and children. Above them, the first star emerged unhurriedly; the wandering star of the evening, finally visible in the indigo sky.

"She loved you," Charles finally said.

"I know," Locky replied, maybe because he knew, or maybe because he just wanted his dad to shut up.

Charles was no longer speaking rehearsed lines, merely allowing the speech to form as it would.

"You were her bright star in the dark night."

He liked to think he momentarily saw the hint of a smile on his son's face, but he could have been wrong. God knew he'd been wrong so many times before.

THIRTY-FOUR

Friday, 15 August 2025

During the night, he slept. He slept in a dreamless
sleep.

THIRTY-FIVE

??2025??

At a certain point along the way, his home changed. Things were not in their usual spot, and other objects seemingly vanished. He missed the old crimson wallpaper, the one with the little avian patterns on it, where he would get lost for hours staring at it with his daughter. *There's a pelican, Dad,* she would say, and he would notice a cockatoo with a crest the size of its body. It must have been his daughter who rearranged the room and his belongings; she had said she would, after her mother had gone, *Dad you should shake things up, it's the best way to move forward.* She was young though, his daughter. Didn't understand the sentiments garnered upon material objects in time. He only wished she might have told him she was going ahead with such big changes, for now he couldn't find the new spot for his house keys, and that nanny the neighbours hired wasn't much cop either. *That nanny must change her hair every day; young folk messing with their hair all the time,* often he thought it was silly, other days he'd have loved to throw a bottle of dye on his scalp and see what the fuss was about. He'd done it once, at his wife's bequest; *too much salt in the pepper these days, why not get that hue back on the noggin', tall dark handsome thing you are.* She often teased him like that, but he wouldn't have had it any other way. *There'll come a day when the kids think we're gross,* she said, *stop holding hands, you're not young flames anymore.* They wouldn't understand the playfulness of a mum and dad married for decades. *Tell me it will be decades.* He would visit the coffee shop every day he could, hoping to catch a glimpse of her behind the machine, her bracelets jangling away like fruit bats on a wire while she worked the grinder. He knew they'd marry one day, meant to be and all that; she'd pour little heart patterns on top of his coffee, flourish the letters of his name with stars as she wrote his order down on the paper cup. *Take me to the moon, my space man.* One day the coffee shop had been closed, burst water main out the front or something like that, and he'd been so distressed when the nanny had found him. He remembered her that day, angry yet relieved to see him, *and my goodness did she give me an earful. Why did she care so much, I can come and get a coffee, damn it;* but the anger subsided into wonderment, for he saw the coffee shop had a new display of tapestry and clothing – *a strange thing to sell in a café, they must be expanding their business;* he knew a lot of people did that these days. Small towns never stayed the same; to be a no-name in a no-name town – could a person be more insignificant than that? *An insignificant miracle, my love.* The nanny wouldn't let him drive home, and he was too tired to argue. *Nice of her to bring in more firewood; measure twice and cut once,* he'd always told his boy. He asked the nanny if he could take a moment, he'd just like to check on his son, he liked to stack toy blocks in his room. The things they'd build together, he the father being invited into his son's little domain, where three blocks could be a skyscraper and a few pieces of wooden track could be the launchpad for rockets into space. *I'll fly all the way to mummy.* But he couldn't find his son's room – just a mass of cardboard boxes covered in dust, and furniture draped in plastic tarps. The nanny would smile patiently and remind him that his son was in the city and would visit soon, she was sure. *Kids and their imagination.* He wondered what pretend-job his son had; moments like that made the hard times worth it. He'd worked his hands to the bone to provide for his children, and they wouldn't know – wouldn't need to know – of the sacrifice a parent makes. *People would pretend all sorts of things,* he thought, *like that strange woman on the phone calling me her dad.* What made folks so crazy? Still, he regretted that one argument he'd had with his boy; he only wanted what was best for his son, and sometimes you just have to trust that your old man knows what he's saying. *Oh son, I just want you to get the most out of yourself – he is so capable, that son of mine.* Why it was that he would ruminate under the frondescence of a poisoned nostalgia, he did not know. Maybe it was just that he wished he could change things here or there, maybe the outcome would have been different, maybe another path taken, maybe tragedy avoided. Truly he hated to hurt people, and the idea that he could even inadvertently let someone down was like a dagger in his heart. There was a time when he'd caught his wife in the bathroom, trying to cut her wrist or something like that, or burn her thigh with a lighter; had he been there a moment earlier, he might have stopped it, but there was no point thinking about that now. He would visit her grave every day he could, present her flowers every day he could. He said for years that it had been all his fault – half his life to be certain. How many other people had their life split directly down the middle by inconceivable horror? Yet maybe he'd live a little longer yet. Should have noticed, pay attention or you'll miss it. As a boy he'd made his mother cry once – if she was still around, he'd apologise for an incident she'd most likely have forgotten. So much time had passed since, water under the bridge, through the channels, out the other side unimpeded – into the sea and evaporated away – why he'd spend so much time recalling that bad memory was a curse he'd spent the latter side of his life trying to manage. It was her, and always would be, his love, his only; he prayed they would reunite one day, that it just took a little stoicism, we'll meet again one day. And at what point did memories simply become dreams? Such distance spread between them; his shoulders shrugged, he didn't know, he was just so tired, and he knew that such fatigue usually meant there'd be a dreamless slumber that evening, with the occasional vignette, void of time or purpose, playing pellucid before his mind's eye. He often hoped that the final sleep would be like that – just a big cauldron of dream memories, like books on a shelf or waves crashing on a beach. He dreamed of a world where everyone was everything they ever were, old and young at the same time, but it hurt to try and comprehend such a paradox. Sometimes he hoped and dreamed nothing at all, for his mind would dull beyond reception, into a somnial tide, and only time would tell if the sleep was eternal. *How funny,* he finally thought, *that time would tell if time* – it made no sense at all.

THIRTY-SIX

Friday, 15 August 2025

"Was going to wander up to Mum's grave before I leave; if you wanted to join. No pressure,"

Lachlan turned from the kitchen window to where Leah stood at the glass doors of the living room.

"Sure," he said, "I reckon I can bear that,"

"Bear it,"

"Huh?"

Leah shook her head, "Nothing. You just reminded me of something Dad said once, a Kipling poem," she clicked her fingers to remember, "I'll get this wrong – *If you can bear to see the things you gave your life to, broken, and stoop and build them up with worn-out tools* – excuse my paraphrasing,"

"Could have fooled me. Beautiful words,"

"Yeah. He was pretty smart, our dad. Probably more philosophical than we ever gave him credit for."

They'd followed the path to the back of the property; watched as the wind glided through the eucalypt trees – once seeds in a time nobody left would remember, and there they'd continued to stand resolute to their lot; further out, the planets continued to spin.

"I never come here," said Lachlan, "I just ignored it. Forgot it was here,"

"You never told anybody; why? Why would you hold that burden to yourself?"

He bent to pull a weed from the ground around the tombstone, throwing it and watching as it caught in the wind.

"She didn't see me. I ran. I've run ever since,"

There was a peculiar lightness for him having shared his suppression, his admission of a deep suffering; the words flowed easily to his trusted sibling, and a new shame laid itself before him.

"I can't believe I didn't know Dad was unwell. I was so caught up in my own head. I can't explain this guilt,"

Leah placed her hand on his shoulder, "Forgive yourself, Lock. Dad would have,"

He shook with sobs, the last remnants of perfume from the grave's wilted flowers cloyed in the morning.

"It's been a weird week. Dad dying sort of overloaded my ability to cope. I just feel so emotionally displaced – void and full to capacity all at once,"

"I'm not going to say everything will miraculously improve overnight," said Leah, "we'll never have all the answers. I guess we can use the pieces we gather from others to shape our outlook. From others like family,"

"Yeah," he said, "Thanks,"

She patted his shoulder and turned back down the hill towards the house.

"See? There's nuggets of wisdom amongst my terrible advice."

Her smile lifted his spirit.

They would wait for Leah's taxi at the bottom of the hill, knowing it would not be long until they returned to the house. It was never the last time. Soon the day would come for them to sort through the old home, through the memories, and choose which bricks they'd keep and which they'd cast aside, and raise their future upon the foundation left by their loving parents. And then would arrive the moment when the house would be sold, passed along to another family to build up or knock down with their own story.

Lachlan watched the sunlight that filtered through the branches, watched the way his sister sat on top of her suitcase and cleaned her nails, mannerisms he found so recognisable from their shared childhood.

"I meant what I said, by the way. That I'll come to South Australia. I'll help you deal with your dramas. I might not be terribly useful, but I'll find a way,"

Leah smiled, "I'd like to see you more often, bro. There's a lot to sort through. I can't just get up and leave. It's going to require patience and a bit of tact. I can't risk it getting bigger than it already is,"

He admired her tolerance but bristled with frustration that the struggles that afflicted her could not be fixed immediately; it seemed impossibly unjust.

"Surely we can't scatter Dad's ashes with *him* standing next you. I think I'm done hiding how I truly feel,"

"It might be the case until the moment comes when I leave him. I need you to understand that. It's best to not poke the hornet nest. Until then, we can just pretend,"

He thought for a moment; he may not have understood her methods, but had to trust she knew the safest route for herself and her daughter. He would wait, and swore himself an oath that he would act when the time came.

"Just pretend," he repeated, "Shouldn't be a problem,"

Leah's phone chimed. The taxi was still a while away.

"They're bloody slow, these blokes,"

"Can I ask something, Lee?"

"What's up,"

"Did you ever feel angry at Mum?"

"Nope. Never substantially, at least. I can't imagine the pain she must have gone through. The best thing we can do is love the life she gave us; we don't have a damn thing without her. It is her gift to me and you. That's what I think anyway,"

She shook her head with frustration.

"There's such a massive pressure on women, on mothers. I don't say that to be some sort of martyr.

The expectation that we'll have it altogether, keep a happy harmony. I want to up and leave that man immediately, but what sort of risk does that put Georgia under? He's already proven what he's capable of, and that's with me staying relatively compliant. I'm stuck playing nice, forced to just bide my time,"

There was a fury burning within Locky, and he searched for an appropriate place to put it. He imagined reacting with violence of his own, yet knew how hypocritical that would be. Life was so wretchedly indifferent – he knew he still had much to learn.

"Maybe," he said, redirecting himself, "we can look at it like a piece of music. It's not all harmony. There's tension and dissonance – ideas that don't sound very pleasant, but the music doesn't function without them. But then you might get a resolution, you can hope for it; well, life's like that,"

"A nice thought," replied Leah, "but that hope for a resolution will need a bit of work to arrive at,"

"And that's what we'll do," he replied defiantly, "I can't wait to meet Georgia,"

"Meet?"

"Yes. She deserves to be introduced to a better version of her uncle,"

Leah laughed quietly, "She loves Halloween. Can you believe that? We never got that as kids — everyone used to say it was 'too American'. But I reckon between you and I there'd be some fun ghost stories to tell,"

"Mate, I wouldn't even need to dress up to be scary."

At last the taxi arrived, the driver having gotten himself lost more than once in the winding back roads of the Southern Highlands. Leah waved him away and put her suitcase into the boot, before giving her brother a swift kiss on the cheek.

"Don't be a stranger,"

"I won't. I promise."

Lachlan watched the car pull away, until the sound of the engine drifted beyond earshot. He breathed deeply of the beautiful morning, the sunshine, the magpies that sung unseen in the branches above. In that moment he stood; with his father on his mind and his mother in his heart, his back turned to the house, facing the wide world beyond the bounds of the property.

"I thank God for a new day."

It wasn't until much later on that he noticed the single, impactful change to his daily devotion.

END

About the author:

P.S.Clinen lives in New South Wales, Australia. He has written several novels and works of poetry and releases music under the name Pinnacle Tricks. All of his works can be found online.

www.psclinen.com